Compelling Evidence

New Detective Stories

Edited by David C. Dougherty

COMPELLING EVIDENCE:
New Detective Stories

Edited by David C. Dougherty

ISBN 978-0-692-80863-4

The *Black Mask* cover photo in the Introduction is reproduced with permission of Keith Deutsch 1943, BlackMask.com.

INQUIRIES
Graduate Program in Liberal Studies
Loyola University Maryland
HU-236C
4501 North Charles Street
Baltimore, MD 21210
liberalstudies@loyola.edu

Contents

Acknowledgements

The editor gratefully notes that the *Black Mask* cover photo in the Introduction is reproduced with permission of Keith Deutsch 1943, BlackMask.com.

Thanks to Dr. Randy Donaldson, Director of the Graduate Program in Liberal Studies Program at Loyola University Maryland, for his consistent and enthusiastic support for this project since 2012. And a special shout-out to Dr. Steven A. Burr, assistant Director of Liberal Studies, who has assisted the editor in bringing the material to copy-readiness and helped with shepherding the files through publication.

But mostly, thanks to nine wonderful students who wrote splendid stories as their class projects, and revised them rigorously for publication, long after the grades were in. And also to their many classmates who didn't publish, whether as a matter of choice or as a result of not being selected, but who may have inspired the writers collected here with comments, encouragement, or friendship, as they often inspired the editor.

Compelling Evidence

Introduction

David C. Dougherty

A few years ago, at my first post-retirement job, the vicar of a nearby Episcopal Church expressed a poplar response to my then-current project, wrapping up a class called "Detective Fiction and Film." The good Doctor immediately exclaimed, "What an exciting class!" But later, when she asked me to share some of the details with her spouse, a lawyer, she had undergone something of a change of heart. Now she questioned the legitimacy of offering a class in Sherlock Holmes over one in Shakespeare. And her husband pretty much agreed. So did a *Baltimore Sun* newspaperman when he interviewed me many years ago on the occasion of the very first, undergraduate, version of this class.

Legitimate question. And for the record, I have offered a Liberal Studies class called Shakespeare and Film, but it has never achieved the enrollments of detective fiction. Not consistently, at least. In 2012 detective fiction closed on the first day of registration, and I can't recall ever delivering this class to a less-than-full enrollment. That time, because of an anomaly in the schedule, it ran with 150% of the maximum enrollment. In 2016 the hybrid version of the class was somewhat slower to close, but it ran at 110% of the recommended maximum enrollment. Although market value is a less than ideal criterion for academic legitimacy, there's something beyond merely reading about Sherlock Holmes that appeals to an intelligent, critical audience of graduate students.

And of course, that's what our classes were about. We read a great deal more – qualitatively as well as quantitatively – than the great British sleuth, and along the way we discovered that the form itself comes out of and reflects values that evolved with the Scientific Revolution. Of course, in *A Study in Scarlet*, John Watson, a physician returned from war in Afghanistan (*plus ca change,* a point brilliantly made in Martin Freeman's portrayal of Watson in the first of the Mark Gattis films in 2011) makes the acquaintance of an idiosyncratic chemist named Holmes. As we read Sir A. Conan Doyle, or Dorothy Sayers, we're invited to share an artistic illusion that the human mind is sufficient to solve all our problems, be they social or even moral. And when it's done well that's the most comforting illusion of them all.

Most of the students, however, found themselves more at home in the native tradition, based not on science but on existential uncertainty. The detective becomes not a superior observer (and, really, some of Holmes's observations which morph into clues are downright silly; many of G. K. Chesterton's Father Brown's are; and Lord Peter, Sayers' aristocratic sleuth, at times actually raises the bar for silly clues, as does Hercule Poirot), but rather a determined seeker for a solution to some specific but elusive mystery – not necessarily truth with a capital T. The supreme value ceases to be scientific objectivity, but rather perseverance, integrity, and the willingness to abide by a code that has no experimental certainty (wouldn't be a code it if did, would it?). Along with a batch of critical apparatus the class studied the "big four" American detective writers (Dashiell Hammett, Raymond Chandler, Ross Macdonald and Robert B. Parker), and filmmakers who tried, with varying results, to bring their creations to the screen without too much dumbing down, as well as two brilliant contemporary writers who bring the question of gender to the enterprise, Sue Grafton and Laura Lippman—perhaps America's answer to the "Queens of Crime"— Sayers, Agatha Christie, Ngaio Marsh and Margery Allingham. After decades of demeaning female stereotypes in both the British and American detective stories, it's gratifying to know that detectives can not only be female, but can compete with their more testosterone-rich cohorts quite successfully. Some, like Grafton's Kinsey Millhone or Sara Peretsky's V. I Warshawski, are every bit as tough as the film noir detective heroes like Phillip Marlowe or Sam Spade. And as we learn in *The Girl in the Green Raincoat* (2008), Tess Monaghan can out-tough the toughest of the Spade-Marlowe-Archer-Spenser crowd – by having a baby.

One assumption guiding our work was the theory that popular culture probably tells us at least as much about ourselves as *haute couture* does. Only the rarest person has her life significantly changed by reading Virginia Woolf, and that person probably has some pretty serious problems if she sees her experience reflected in Woolf's brilliant characters, rhetoric, and situations. But in the world of pop culture, we often experience what Herman Melville called "the shock of recognition." For many of us, seeing our beloved, broken Baltimore

Cover for an edition of Black Mask, *an historically important pulp fiction magazine founded by H. L. Mencken and George Jean Nathan and later edited by Col. Joseph Shaw, that published many of the early American detective writers including Hammett and Chandler. Col. Shaw's emphasis on "redeeming social importance" differentiated* Black Mask *from many of its competitors, and provided a sharp contrast to its often-lurid content. It set the tone for the bridge between pop culture and haute couture that characterized the American detective writers. This particular cover is the artwork of Raphael DeSoto. Photo reproduced by permission, Keith Deutsch 1948, www.blackmask.com.*

through Lippman's eyes in *Butchers Hill* was a revelation of the many problems we all face, and of the humor, idiosyncrasy, and even decency that lurks behind the crime statistics and headlines. And although that point has the liability of being another quantitative argument – many more people read Robert B. Parker than James Joyce, who, in this country at least, is read mostly by students who have assignments to complete – there's a current of truth behind it as well. We see our times and our conditions reflected in the fictions people actually consume.

The principal assignment for this class was the creation of an original detective story, using and building on the formulas as the great detective writers have done. The goal was to make students aware, though practice, how hard it is to write a really good detective story, whether of the cerebral or the existential sort. And how very much revision is needed to hide the clues almost successfully, to bring the resolution to a surprising and satisfying conclusion. Many of the students learned a lot from the assignment, but some—nearly a third of each class—produced stories that, with successive revisions, deserve to be read, partly because they showcase the talents and determination of Liberal Studies students at Loyola. These folks revised and revised and revised long after they got their A's. But mostly, because they're really good.

The story closest to the British tradition is "The Sacrifice of Isaac," at times an homage to and at others a send-up of and even at times a critique of Victorian society and the detective yarns it spun. Katalin Szoboszlay Navarro's British sleuth story doesn't contain a private detective, but, like Charles Dickens and Wilkie Collins (whom we backgrounded) "The Sacrifice of Isaac" features a Scotland Yard Inspector at odds with his immediate superior and sent on a simple mission whose outcome is politically predetermined. But Inspector Edgewood finds a much more complicated situation than he was supposed to, and has a somewhat sexist interchange with a wannabe coroner who complicates his world socially as well as scientifically. Rich in false clues and unexpected turns, "Isaac" at times emulates the complex web of clues in Doyle or Christie. Much like Doyle at his best, Katalin both longs for the stability of the Victorian world and recognizes that *noblesse oblige* wasn't always so noblesse. Her manor hall is preoccupied with respectability, but the reality Inspector Edgewood uncovers before the final unexpected plot twist introduces a considerably more complex, interesting, and worrisome reality behind the manor facade.

Also in the tradition of the great British sleuths of the turn of the twentieth century, Helen Hufford's heroine isn't a detective at all, but a gifted amateur like Sayers' Lord Peter or Chesterton's Fr. Brown. Herself a high school teacher, Hufford creates Ginny Kane as a working mom with two part-time jobs, one as a teacher of photojournalism in a girls' high school and the other as a journalist for a community newspaper. In this Hufford may be influenced by Baltimore's own Lippman, whose "Accidental detective" turned to sleuthing after the newspaper on which she worked went out of business. Kane has amassed a reputation as the school's resident sleuth, using her powers of observation and digging beyond the obvious to help the assistant principal discover truants, vandals, cheaters and the like. In the case before us, Kane also has a vested interest in solving the crime. As she works through this plot, Hufford connects the trivial matter of a missing memory card with the larger, troubling, issue of controlling boyfriends, and with a background narrative that is tragic rather than trivial.

New Jersey native Nicole Stout combines the cerebral with the existential, positioning her point of view with the client, who has a complicated relationship with both her missing lover and the detective she consults to track him down. It's a complex world of underworld connections -- Adriana's missing lover and the detective are both mob-connected, and she freely confesses that she's a "goomata" who has a token hostess job at a restaurant that serves the mob; as a kept woman she keeps a Cadillac, a high-end apartment, and a designer cat named, of course, Fido.

With all this emphasis on Mafia culture in New Jersey, including an amusing scene in which Adriana and her detective hide out in a closet while some of the leaders of the local Mafia eat and meet to discuss business, one might expect a story reminiscent of *The Sopranos*. But while "Canary" has some of the association of luxury and a life of crime associated with the cable television show and its predecessor, *The Godfather* movie franchise, the story relates to the British sleuth tradition by virtue of its clever clues and complex mystery. Adriana, not her detective, recognizes the key clue in the office of a vet for discerning cats, and the mystery's solution creates, not the despair of a Chandler novel or stories in this collection by Carl Kinkel, Jon Richmond, and Jason Brown, but actually a love story reminiscent of a Holmes yarn like "The Boscombe Valley Mystery," or "The Adventure of the Abbey Grange." Though the denouement of "Where's the Canary?" might shock the pious Victorians of Sherlock's time, it's a modern version of an ancient narrative, the triumph of true love.

With a delightful nod to Jim Croce adorning the tile, Dan Helwig's "Hannon, Inc: The Case of the Cat Lady and the Junkyard Dog" locates the detective in a strange environment, with an unusual path to sleuthing. Hannon sets up shop in Slade Mountain, PA – a far cry from Chandler's L.A. or Parker's Boston, though Helwig is clearly influenced by both in deploying the deft verbal quip as a strategy for aggression. We're reminded that the detective tale is essentially an urban allegory, a narrative of redeeming the city and restoring those values on which civilization rests, whether Sherlock copes with decadent aristocrats or the emerging crime syndicates, or Marlowe makes his way through a dying civilization where the mean streets pose dangers to everyone's lives and souls. Helwig attempts something we find in Holmes at his best – the story of the village exposed to the corruptions that have blighted the city.

And Hannon realizes it's not a good way to make a decent living. A divinity student in his undergraduate days -- how many detectives besides Chesterton's Fr. Brown can we say that about? – Hannon embraced his student job in security, and restores Dodge Darts on the side. But in "Hannon Inc" we see that corruption can come to small-town America through that most enlightening of institutions – the university.

As we move from the British prototype toward the American, a much darker world space and world view provides the context for Jonathan Richmond's "The Float," a smarmy Baltimore of gentlemen's clubs, divorce lawyers, and short-term payday loans. One minor character is so bereft of meaning that she welcomes an interview with a phony *Sun* Journalist, hoping for what Andy Warhol dubbed her fifteen minutes of fame. Himself an economics teacher, Richmond connects the practice of "floating" bad checks with the 2008-09 economic melt-down that so completely undermined America's economy, and ultimately with a pessimistic view of our shared existential condition. His detective wanders to Bethany Beach, Delaware, where the lucky ones hide behind gated communities from the consequences of their avarice, while those cashing checks at Lexington Market have to bear those consequences daily and exhibit baseball bats and sidearms to deter robbers, to learn more about his missing banker and the Mercedes with the vanity plate. Like much of the better crime fiction we studied during the semester, Richmond's story deals with the ubiquity of material greed, and the devastating effects this has on our community and ultimately our souls.

Most private detectives in American literature are ex-policemen, often, like Chandler's Marlowe, having been fired for insubordination. One, Lippman's Monaghan, is an ex-journalist. Robert B. Parker's Spenser is both an ex-cop and an ex-prizefighter. But not many are ex-baseball players. Mathematician Chris Panzarella's "Out at Home" successfully combines two literary/pop culture subsets, the detective story and sports fiction. With the murder of a detested owner of a fictional baseball team, Panzarella's Mark Nelson, though he has suppressed (not quite successfully) his past as a ballplayer, gets access to information the police have to struggle for because the community of ballplayers and coaches still trusts him as one of their own. And, as is true in so many American detective stories, the police and the press have credibility problems with the athletes.

But as he digs into the team owner's murder, Nelson probes one of the staples of American sports fiction, the tension between patrician owners and proletarian players and coaches – a motif central to Bernard Malamud's *The Natural* (1952) and the 1984 Barry Levinson film. Upon hearing about the murder, Nelson quips that the list of suspects might include all the Bayhawks' fans because it is widely believed that the owner is more interested in his profit margin than in the team's fortunes. In a clever scene in a public library Nelson uncovers the clue that cracks the case, and in doing so once again invokes a core motif of sports fiction, the tension between the organic or natural and the technological.

Many detective stories begin with an apparently simple problem undertaken by the hero, one that often escalates into a more profound and serious problem lurking behind the original challenge. This is true of most of the stories in the collection, but in none more centrally than Jennifer Louden's "Sliding Into Darkness," which begins as another banal cheating husband search, but evolves into a thoughtful discussion of coerced criminal behavior in the contemporary city, in this case our nation's capital.

Like most of the female detectives of the late twentieth century, Louden's Nina Langston faces problems that relate to gender. Grafton's, Peretsky's, and Lippman's heroines are at pains to explain exactly how she came into the detective business. Many of their elder male counterparts were, like Marlowe, ex-cops who were fired for, or quit the force. Langston came by a quite different route from canine cop to entrepreneur, though like Monaghan she loves her "pups." Like Monaghan and especially Millhone, she trains religiously to stay mentally and physically fit; and even more than both she plays by her own rules, stealing evidence and using disguise as needed to unravel the crimes at the center of this well-plotted narrative. Finally, like Millhone and Monaghan, her male supporters present romantic and sexual complications; before Parker and James Lee Burke, the American detective avoided romantic entanglements, though Archer and even Marlowe were tempted to make permanent romantic arrangements. In *The Poodle Springs Mystery,* Marlowe married a woman he fell for in the brilliant *The Long Goodbye*; but even Parker's efforts to finish Marlowe's final novel didn't save it from a tangled mediocrity. The American female detective writers, including Louden, navigate a much more complex narrative about the relations of love and detecting.

"Vengeance is Mine . . . saith the Lord" (Romans 12:19 and Leviticus 9:18; and Mickey Spillane, who used that allusion to title his third novel). Almost all Spillane's bloody, sensational narratives attempt to legitimate Mike Hammer's searches for vengeance. And it's the subject of one of the greatest detective tales ever spun, though that detective has no training and is a prince. But Hamlet has to figure out whether a crime has actually been committed, and by whom – and he's aware of the complication that he really wants a reason to go after Claudius, and proof of murder will do very well to validate his innate desire to harm the villain who bedded his mom and stole his dad's kingdom. As Hamlet assimilates compelling evidence that the ghost isn't lying after all, Shakespeare turns the sordid tale of vengeance he inherited from *Historica Danica* (and an extant play, possibly by Thomas Kyd) into a profound meditation on the moral issues and imperatives associated with revenge.

And revenge figures in many a detective yarn, though usually it's the client or the villain seeking corporal revenge, not the detective—though Sherlock loves nothing more than putting one over on "that imbecile Lestrade," as he once called the inspector he considered the least incompetent among the Scotland Yard force. Army vet Carl Kinkel's "It Needed Doing" takes a dark view of revenge, and uses a fascinating variation on the point of view—in this case the putative audience – to consider large and troubling social issues, such as drunken driving and official complicity in keeping repeat drunk drivers out of jail, and covering up DUI offenses. His detective uses a particularly clever means of coercion to get at the crime behind the crime which strikes the hero very closely.

By far the darkest vision in the book is Jason Brown's "Max Parker." The story blends the pessimism of Chandler and his mentor Ernest "Winner take Nothing" Hemingway, as well as the ambiance of cinema noir, which found amenable narratives (and screenwriters) among America's detective writers, with the even darker, post-modern nihilism of graphic novelists like Frank Miller. Perhaps it's the final scene, but the cynicism of *Sin City* seems to pervade "Max Parker." It's also a take on the mean streets Chandler so eloquently defined, with whores, druggies, crooked doctors, and union bosses who preside over criminal trafficking.

Chandler famously said that "down these mean streets a man must go who is himself neither mean nor afraid" and concludes that the essential quality of the realistic detective novel—as opposed to the whodunit—is honor. But it seems a stretch, perhaps post-modernly so, to think of Max as a man of honor. He's a burned-out-case, a former DEA agent who went rogue after being betrayed by his nemesis, Big Charlie, and serving time. Parker's status as a felon, who therefore cannot get a license as a private detective or a carry permit, presents challenges Brown cleverly meets. But Parker's status is fluid, and that's where the post-modernist angst comes in. He's both the detective and the hunted; the person who finds the missing prescription pad and the man who wants and needs illegal drugs; the naïve idealist about the love of an ex-whore and the enraged avenger when he can't escape the fact that her sexual favors were a means of playing him; and a vigilante who plays god when all the systems fail. Whereas Marlowe confesses, in *The Big Sleep*, that he's (and we're) "part of the nastiness now," Parker emulates Huck Finn and "lights out for the territory" in a boat he bought with ill-got gains, a small slush fund (ditto) and a few days' supply of painkiller. We're left to wonder, at the story's end, how far any of it is going to get him.

* * * * *

Compelling evidence—the ideal for every detective story. We know from historical evidence that in the real world, many crimes remain unsolved; and the Innocence Project and other like-minded organizations, aided by new technologies, often DNA, have shown convincingly that far too many people serve time, or even die, for crimes someone else committed. But that's the real world. And the comforting illusion detective fiction provides is that it doesn't have to be that way. For me, however, the compelling evidence is that the recognized illusion admonishes us to strive for a more just world; and that there's a lot of compellingly evident new talent out there, and in these pages. And by the way: it's not an accident that the typeface for this collection is Baskerville!

So here they are—nine of the finest from two very different classes that learned, in quite different ways, that there's a lot more than Sherlocking to this stuff – even if most of us learned to admire the Cumberbatch/Freeman modernization of the great British detective and Lucy Liu as Watson in a successful television series, though most were surprised to learn that Rex Stout once wrote a tongue-in-cheek essay "proving" that Watson was a woman. They learned that in the hands of Chandler, Macdonald, or Lippman, the formula becomes a way to bridge the gap between popular narrative and serious literature. And they've achieved quite a lot by bridging it for themselves.

The Sacrifice of Isaac

Katalin Szoboszlay Navarro

It was evening-time, not long after the servants retired. The candles flickered in the East Wing. Mrs. Cox, the esteemed housekeeper of Green Brier, tucked her ashen hair into her nightcap. There was still much work to be done. After she drew the silk curtains, she began to dust, with reverent attention, the portraits and marble bust of her Master, Lord Walter Herringbone. For over twenty-seven years, Mrs. Cox kept the candlesticks shining and her Master appeased. Thus the Lord praised her often for her punctuality, orderliness, and most importantly, her discretion. He had particular reason to cherish this quality. In the hardships that befell Green Brier, she was resilient and firm. Mrs. Cox was, as Sir Walter often remarked, "of sturdy stock."

Perhaps that is why when gunshot erupted from upstairs, Mrs. Cox sounded no alarm. She was not the least surprised, though her hand trembled slightly. "Thank goodness the servants have gone in for the night," she whispered, praying the storm had masked the shots. She grabbed a candle to investigate. Upon reaching the Master's study, she noticed the door was slightly ajar. Mrs. Cox momentarily experienced what can only be described as gratitude she had not been present when it happened. Her stifled breathing caught her by surprise. "Have some nerve," she muttered, and turned the brass knob.

Sir Walter lay sideways on the maroon and gold stitched carpet, the Lancaster pistol in hand. His eyes were placidly closed, almost peaceful. Droplets of blood still freshly resided in his white sideburns. At the sight of his brains dashed against the wall, Mrs. Cox's knees buckled.

Had she covered not her mouth, her screams would have alerted the entire household. The sight was more grisly than she had prepared for. Yet Mrs. Cox was, as her Master himself claimed, "of sturdy stock." She gnawed at her fingers to sharpen her wits, and steadied herself upon the writing desk. Mrs. Cox's sunken eyes found their way to the cracked parchment:

> My dearest wife:
> I can bear no more of this life. I have squandered all that

we had. The little I have left I give to my dear Isaac. I leave you my love in utter shame and dishonour. I only ask that you send for Isaac to return home from his studies immediately. He will be of more use to you now. I beg your forgiveness and God's mercy. Walt

Mrs. Cox read the note several times before carefully folding it into her pocket. "I wish you hadn't done it," she remarked sadly, "but I understand why." After locking the door, she swiftly descended into the servants' quarters. A solitary lamp revealed the grim faces of the awakened servants.

"Our Master," Mrs. Cox began in a weak voice, "has had a most tragic accident. Pray, do not ask me anything tonight. I insist you all return to your rooms at once. Mr. Scrivener, come with me."

The housekeeper and footman silently paced down the aisle, until the rest were out of earshot.

"Charles, he has finally done it."

"Ma'am?"

"Telegraph the Police. This must be handled with the *utmost* delicacy."

"Then it was no accident Mrs. Cox?" Mr. Scrivener stooped lower to whisper. "Are you sure?"

"You know the answer as well as I. Do as I ask. Pay what you must. If you hurry, they should arrive by tomorrow afternoon or day after at latest." Mr. Scrivener's voice squeaked, "Mrs. Cox!"

"We don't have much time—"

"Was it with her father's pistol?"

"Yes, the Lancaster."

"God rest his soul."

February 1884

"You're late, Mr. Edgewood," the Chief barked, lighting his pipe. "I'm rather surprised, given your excellent references."

"The train was late actually," the dark-haired man replied. The Constable observed he was of strong constitution, with a clean-shaven face, and remarkably even teeth. He recognized immediately from his bearing that he had been an officer.

"I'll be frank with you, Mr. Edgewood," he puffed. "I don't tolerate excuses. Perhaps that is how it is done in the *Navy*, but not here. Former officers like yourself are all the same: full of excuses. Yet they all believe they deserve a position." Mr. Edgewood guessed that the Constable did not take kindly to officers, and thus responded with a knowing smile.

"Well of course I deserve a position, sir," he grinned.

The Constable blew the smoke forcefully into his face. "The majority of men in this country are not worthy of the Constabulary. Drunkenness, licentiousness, it's enough to make any man say to hell with it and retire to the country. Since you seem so very confident as to your abilities, I think I have just the case for you. I received a telegram this morning from Constable Chadwick in Sussex that I think you might find very interesting. It's an accidental shooting case. Fact is there are rumors of suicide, and the gentleman, Lord Walter Herringbone, was highborn. You know how these vicars handle burial of suicides. Naturally the family doesn't want to publicize anything to taint the family's reputation."

"Can't their local Constables handle such matters?" Mr. Edgewood inquired. The Constable extinguished his pipe with precision, imagining, with great satisfaction, how quickly Mr. Edgewood would fail. It pleased him to humble an officer. "These are unusual circumstances, Mr. Edgewood. You're right; it's usually not within our jurisdiction. However, Constable Chadwick is indisposed at present. He's investigating a much more urgent matter."

"More urgent than the death of a gentleman?" Edgewood inquired.

"I'm giving you a chance here, Edgewood," the Chief chided, "or are you all arrogance with nothing to show for it?" He removed a piece of lint from his uniform. Mr. Edgewood's lip twitched in annoyance, sensing he had other motives. "I suppose I shall go then, seeing as Constable Chadwick is so very . . . indisposed. The task you've given is quite simple really. I daresay almost too simple. In fact, I'd wager you'd want this to be as quick and clean as possible. I suppose you'd prefer for me to lie on my report, as it would be more expedient for all parties. Suppose there's more money in it for you too."

The Constable folded his hands. "Lord Herringbone was a very elderly man . . . *accidents* happen all the time."

"My honor compels me to report truthfully, sir. You could say the *Navy* taught me that."

The Chief gave him a pained smile. "Well then failure is impossible. Train leaves at eleven. You wouldn't want to miss that."

Green Brier had been, by most accounts, one of the finest estates in Sussex. One says 'had been' because few of the gentility called upon Sir Walter and his beautiful young wife since the onset of his mysterious illness. The Lady of the house was still a ripe age, twenty-five. Lady Grace had been married to Sir Walter about three years, and their marriage was thought to have been quite happy. At one time, Green Brier entertained some of the most gifted artists, philosophers, and poets of the time. This was no doubt due to Lady Grace's influence. Yet Green Brier was most celebrated for its great beauty and close proximity to the warm summer seas. At present, her Ladyship was en route to Bath with a friend. Unfortunately, Sir Walter was too ill to accompany her on this particular holiday. It was just as well, as the doctor had prescribed for the ailing Lord ample bed-rest and, of course, the Sussex sunshine.

Mr. Edgewood knocked thrice on the heavy iron knocker, and was received by a stout, frumpy woman. "You must be the Constable from London," Mrs. Cox remarked. "Please come in."

"Thank you Ma'am," he replied, removing his hat. "Please, Mr. Edgewood would do just fine for now."

"As you wish, sir. I'm sorry our footman is not here to receive you. We've short-staffed as of late, due to recent dismissals."

Mr. Edgewood's ears perked up. "Dismissals?"

"Yes, Consta—I mean, Mr. Edgewood. There are only five servants left."

"That's a very small staff considering the size of the property," he admitted. "How were the dismissed servants deficient?"

Mrs. Cox tempered her response. "There was evidence to believe they were thieves, sir."

"Is that what the local constable concluded?"

"Why would we call upon Constable Chadwick? We felt we had sufficient evidence."

Mr. Edgewood grimaced. "I suppose that's the way everything is done here in the country."

"Quite so," Mrs. Cox agreed. "We do have a particular way about doing things!"

Mr. Edgewood looked displeased. "If it's not too much an inconvenience Ma'am . . . can you take me to the scene?"

"I wish you wouldn't put it like that Mr. Edgewood. 'The scene.' You don't look the queasy sort, but —"

"I'm not as queasy as some, Ma'am," he interrupted.

Mrs. Cox nodded solemnly. "Nor am I, Mr. Edgewood."

The Constable didn't bother to coax the housekeeper inside. He knew she wouldn't enter the study without firm nudging. Mr. Edgewood observed that the flies had already begun to settle on the corpse. He knew the smell would soon follow.

"Is this how you found him?" She gave a short jerk of the head, looking away.

"And you were alone?"

"Yes, all the s-s-ervants were in their beds. I heard no one else, sir. No one."

"And there was a storm, was there not, Mrs. Cox?"

She nervously straightened her cap. "Yes, Constable, it was a thunderous evening."

"Then let me clarify: is it possible someone may have slipped by undetected as you were ascending the stairs?"

"I'd have heard or seen someone, Mr. Edgewood," she grunted. "I am always vigilant!"

Mr. Edgewood rubbed his hands together, noticing the toppled books and papers scattered about the floor. He considered the possibility of a struggle. "Were the books like that when you found him?"

"I believe so. I don't know precisely," she remarked. Mr. Edgewood scribbled more notes. She didn't like it. "Really Mr. Edgewood, why would I take time to look about? The sight of the Master's body was quite enough for this old woman."

The Constable squinted as if to ascertain whether or not the housekeeper was being genuine. "These spinster types are most difficult," he thought, kneeling down to observe the bullet wound. "Has the body been moved in any way whatsoever?"

"Heavens, no! Who would move the body? Only her Ladyship and I have the key, and she has been away." The housekeeper cleared her throat. "But I feel I should mention that the door was ajar when I found it."

"Why were the books scattered?" he asked her. She shrugged her shoulders. "I s-s-suppose the Master was blasted backwards from the force of the discharge. Bullets ricochet and so forth," Mrs. Cox explained, as if this was a new idea to Constable.

"No gun would be powerful enough to throw these books about. Did he have any enemies?"

She snorted in contempt. "Not one. And I would know, I have worked for him for over twenty-seven years!"

Mr. Edgewood looked up from his notebook. "What about those he recently dismissed?"

"I should think not. They all found other employment without delay. At least equal to their former pay. He was a good Master—never prone to fits of temper."

The Constable ruffled his hair. "Do you have any idea why he'd have a gun in a personal library?"

Mrs. Cox scoffed. "What would I know of my Master's proclivities?"

"Well, I just assumed, since you worked for him for over twenty years." Her nose flushed.

"That may be so, but I have no explanation for why he would have been using the gun. Perhaps he wished to clean it?"

Mr. Edgewood examined the gun carefully without touching it. "It's a fine weapon," he admired. "It's quite popular in India."

"Accidental misfire seems unlikely," he thought. "Was there any note, Mrs. Cox?"

Her eyes flashed. "A note, Mr. Edgewood?"

"Yes, Mrs. Cox, a note. Some indication of a goodbye?"

"Certainly not. I shall tell you again, Mr. Edgewood, this was a most unfortunate accident."

"When shall your Mistress be returning?"

"Tomorrow I believe," she answered. "I sent word for her."

"Has the gentleman any children?"

"Yes, one son. Ten years old. He's away at school at present."

"And when will he return?"

"That is for the Mistress to decide." She wearily rubbed her eyes.

"I think I should like to take tea now, Mrs. Cox."

The parlour was a smartly decorated room, with a marble stone fireplace and a plush overstuffed sofa. "While we're waiting for our tea, Mrs. Cox . . . I've a few more questions if you can bear it. Before I begin, have you sent for the coroner yet?"

"Do you think me a dunce, Mr. Edgewood," she retorted. "You think I want a foul stench in my house? Yes, I sent for him. He should be here within the hour."

"My dear Mrs. Cox, I would never insult a woman of your particular qualities," he said playfully. "You are indeed one of the most capable women I have become acquainted with in the whole of my police career."

The housekeeper was not amused. "You give me a most excessive compliment, sir, for I believe you must be acquainted with indeed many exceptional ladies."

Mr. Edgewood grinned, revealing a distinct dimple in his right cheek. "I'd never admit to it."

After a few minutes of silence, Miss Mortimer entered carrying a silver tray and rose-painted teacups. The cook meticulously poured the tea so that it was just below the teacup's rim. From the angle at which the Constable was sitting, he could see Miss Mortimer was wholesome, perhaps pretty. He guessed her to be about thirty. She avoided his eyes, instead focusing on how much sugar to pour into his teacup.

"You must excuse her," Mrs. Cox piped up, "We have not received visitors in a long time, much less a Constable. Usually she is down in the kitchens, but has taken up more responsibilities within the main house. Entertaining people makes her nervous."

"I don't mind the least," Mr. Edgewood remarked, thanking the woman. "The tea is wonderful."

"Thank you, sir," Miss Mortimer mumbled. "I am glad it's to your tastes." She curtseyed pitifully. Something in her expression compelled Mr. Edgewood to offer condolences.

"I'm very sorry to hear about your Master, Miss." The teacups on her tray wavered slightly.

"A most unfortunate accident," she said evenly.

"Is that what Mrs. Cox told you to say?" Mrs. Cox shot the cook a warning glance. "Mrs. Cox has not instructed us to say anything particular, sir."

Mr. Edgewood took a sip of tea. "How long have you been working here, Miss?"

"About eleven years, sir."

"And your Master was good to you?" Miss Mortimer steadied the teacups with one hand.

"Of course he was good to her," Mrs. Cox interjected. "He most certainly was."

"I sense Miss Mortimer may hold a different opinion," Mr. Edgewood observed.

The cook looked at her feet. "Since you have inquired, sir –"

"Miss Mortimer," Mrs. Cox hissed.

"Let her speak," Mr. Edgewood insisted.

The woman's voice quivered. "I-I-I am sure you realize the peculiar circumstances of our recently dismissed staff. They were not relieved of their position for any substantial reasons. T-T-That is to say –"

"They couldn't afford to keep them on. I've concluded as much," Mr. Edgewood finished.

"I'm sorry to admit it sir. The Master's vices took a toll on all the staff, the Mistress particularly," she confessed.

Mrs. Cox was appalled. Mr. Edgewood gestured for silence. "It's understandable why Mrs. Cox would rather keep the financial matters of the estate private. I don't blame you for your discretion, Mrs. Cox. Your loyalty to your Master is admirable." Mrs. Cox wiped her spectacles with a linen handkerchief. "You have done enough for today, Ruth. You may go." The cook excused herself.

"I will speak to my Mistress about this. I'll have her dismissed," she muttered. "Insolent, opinionated girl!"

Mr. Edgewood laid the teacup on the table. "I don't think that would be wise, Mrs. Cox. Everyone needs a cook." She sneered. Mr. Edgewood continued, "However, Miss Mortimer did present some intriguing points about your Master's habits. How was his mood in recent months? Did he seem distracted? Indifferent? Perhaps depressed? Severe changes in circumstances often lead to the worst melancholy." The housekeeper did not answer at first, but she knew the Constable was patient. He would wait for her response, *ad infinitum*.

"The Master, through no fault of his own, had come upon financial hardship." Mr. Edgewood ruffled his hair again. When in deep contemplation, Robert Edgewood often had the habit of ruffling his wavy hair. Some may have thought it was from vanity. The truth of the matter was that it improved his concentration. He knew he would have to breach this subject delicately. "I know your Master was taken ill for quite some time, Ma'am. Was he prescribed opium?"

"Do not insult us so gravely, Mr. Edgewood!"

"Well, what were the vices Miss Mortimer was speaking of? Women?"

Mrs. Cox yelped in protest. "Who would want for anything when he has the most beautiful wife in the county! Our mistress, Lady Grace, is as enchanting as any I have ever laid eyes upon. It was never women," she hissed. "It was cards. Please do not speak of it. I forbid anyone to do so in my presence."

"Gambling is a common enough habit, Ma'am. Have you any knowledge of any outstanding debts?"

"What an idea! The Master never made any of us privy to those sorts of affairs."

"Let those who have ears, hear, Ma'am. I know how these matters unfold."

"I do no such eavesdropping. My Lord hired me for my discretion." Mrs. Cox continued smoothing her skirts, desperately wishing the conversation to end. She could not tell him of the letter. The Mistress wouldn't like it.

"Is there anything else, Mrs. Cox?"

The butler knocked upon the door. "I'm sorry for interrupting Ma'am. But there's a message for you. Seems the coroner has taken ill, but is sending his assistant."

"An apprentice? I didn't even know he had one." The butler told her to expect the gentleman within the hour.

"Let us hope he arrives before Lady Grace returns home. She faints from the mere sight of blood. Smelling salts only do so much good for silly girls."

Miss Frances Burrows had already pricked her finger several times with the needle. Sewing is not an easy endeavor while riding in a carriage. Yet she felt resolved to finish her handiwork as a gift for her father. Miss Frances was the only daughter of Doctor Peter Burrows, Sussex coroner. Her mother had perished long before in a smallpox epidemic, and thus it was only the two of them in their small cottage by the sea. Having once been a vigorous fellow, the Doctor refused any apprentices. Thus Frances was the only one to listen to the exacting methods of his profession. And Frances, oddly enough, enjoyed it. Recently, the Doctor confined himself to his room to prevent his daughter from contracting his serious illness. As such, Miss Burrows took it upon herself to carry out his duties to the best of her ability, which is why she felt compelled to answer this house call.

"I do hope that the Lady isn't at home," she thought. She wiped the perspiration off her forehead with the outside of her palm. Frances had never been to such a grand estate, much less spoken to someone of higher station. "I've never lied to a Lady before," she realized. Ladies are taught never to lie, unless of course, it was for their own benefit. It should be said that Miss Burrows had never engaged in deceits like this before. She was an attractive woman of most exemplary character. However, she was unlike most women her age, having preferred reading to elegant balls. In truth, she rarely left home. Yet, given her father's ill health, she felt obliged to come immediately to Green Brier to offer her services. "What would Papa say?" she wondered. "Perhaps he'd find it rather funny to see the looks on their faces." She put the sewing needle and cloth back into her bag. The carriage turned to pass the rusted iron gates. "Here I am, Green Brier," she whispered. "I've come to help you. Yes . . . I realize this is a shock. No, my father has no apprentices. There is no one else who can come. I'm more qualified than anyone in two counties . . . yes, I'm a woman. Are you surprised?"

The wooden carriage spokes crackled against the cobblestone. Mrs. Cox jumped up from the sofa. A veiled woman in a black mourning gown stood before her in the doorway. She extended her thin white hand. "Lady Grace," Mrs. Cox squawked. "I thought, I thought—"

Despite the obscuring veil, Mr. Edgewood gathered this was the Mistress of the house.

"We stopped in Southampton, Mrs. Cox. I came back as soon as I heard–"

"Where is your companion?" Mrs. Cox inquired.

"My . . . oh yes, I had her dismissed." The housekeeper cleared her throat. "Dismissed, my Lady?" "Mrs. Cox, I'm sure you can see I'm quite exhausted. I don't have time to discuss dismissed servants. Have Ruth send up some tea and those scones I–" Her mouth stopped at the presence of the dashing Constable. "Who is this handsome gentleman?" she exclaimed.

"My Lady," huffed Mrs. Cox, "I feel it's not really the proper time to—"

The Lady threw her hands about wildly. "Mrs. Cox, I insist on a proper introduction!"

Mrs. Cox bit her lips. "May I present the Constable of the Metropolitan police, Mr. Edgewood."

"Edgewood," Lady Grace cooed, offering her hand. "It might seem a wild guess, but I suspect you may have been an officer?"

Mr. Edgewood politely kissed her hand. "What gave it away, my Lady?"

"The dimple, naturally." She giggled, throwing back her veil. Mrs. Cox looked mortified.

"I'm sorry for your loss," he replied solemnly. "I see how difficult your husband's death is for you."

"It has destroyed me completely, sir," she whined, loosely swaying. "Oh, I feel weak! Help me Mr. Edgewood," she said breathlessly. A quiet knocking silenced her. "Who could that be?" she asked.

"It must be Burrows' apprentice," Mrs. Cox replied, opening the door. The chestnut-haired woman was looking down at her dress, frantically trying to brush off the dirt. It took her a moment to realize that everyone's eyes were on her. The stranger curtseyed in embarrassment before Mrs. Cox. "Am I addressing the lady of the house?"

Lady Grace cackled, her golden curls jostling. Nevertheless, the Mistress maintained a cautious eye on her housekeeper. "Well, Mrs. Cox? *Are* you now the Lady of the house?" she asked warningly.

Mrs. Cox snorted in contempt. "She must be mad, my Lady."

Miss Burrows cried, "I sincerely meant no offense!" Mr. Edgewood suppressed a chuckle.

"My dear girl," Mrs. Cox quipped. "I do not know *who* you are, but you must be new to Green Brier." "That I am Ma'am, but I am no stranger to the county. We live about thirty miles down the road. I'm

Doctor Burrows' daughter. Unfortunately, he has been suffering from serious illness as of late, and thus has sent me in his absence."

Mrs. Cox frowned. "You must be joking."

"I'm afraid not," the young woman replied, with slight desperation in her voice. "I assure you I've watched my father's practice these past twenty years. I'm quite comfortable examining the deceased. I don't wish to trouble your household at such a difficult time. With your permission, I'd like to briefly examine his remains and be on my way."

Lady Grace waved her hand dismissively. "I have no wish to see him, so retrieve him."

"But my Lady," Mrs. Cox cried. "It is not proper!"

"Don't be so defensive, Mrs. Cox," she replied.

Mr. Edgewood turned back to the Mistress. "With your permission my Lady...I might provide my assistance to Miss Burrows. I doubt she can carry your late husband by herself."

Miss Burrows shot him a look of defiance. "I can manage on my own, I assure you."

Mr. Edgewood smiled. "I insist."

Miss Burrows could see he was quite stubborn. "As you wish," she replied tersely.

Lady Grace looked displeased. "Mrs. Cox, where is Mr. Scrivener?"

"I have been wondering the very same, Ladyship."

"In that case, call upon Sir Thomas Pryce yourself. I wish to inform him of his friend's accident. Miss Burrows," Lady Grace remarked, grabbing her hand. "Take good care of our dear Mr. Edgewood. Be sure you return him to me...in one piece."

When a man has no place to go, he often finds himself in a chapel. Mr. Charles Scrivener found himself in such a position. He didn't care to help the vicar of Sussex wash stained glass windows. Instead the footman stared intently at the Reverend's large, rough hands, a result of tending to the parish himself. At the moment, Reverend Josiah Knightley was trying to prevent the wet cloth from dripping onto the floor. Mr. Scrivener couldn't help but think it was a pointless endeavor. "Have you decided to tell me yet, Charles?"

"I think not, Reverend. I have reasons for withholding." The Reverend sat himself on the pew beside him.

"It will weigh lighter on your soul," the Reverend offered. "Much like washing dirt off a window. Light cannot shine through muddy darkness. But when the glass is clean, much like the soul, the light of God can enter in."

"I cannot go back to Green Brier," Mr. Scrivener declared in a strained voice.

"You've yet to explain why."

"Reverend, if you only knew why I could not…"

"I suspect this pertains to the recent death of your Master," Josiah said gently.

"So you've heard."

"The whole town has heard, Charles."

"They have heard it was an *accident*," Mr. Scrivener corrected.

"Was it?"

"I cannot say."

The vicar slumped over, his hands folded in prayer. "What reasons have you to withhold it?" Josiah asked earnestly.

"My conscience prevents me from revealing it."

"Then let me tell the truth for you. Your conscience will be clear."

"It was not an accident, Reverend."

"So was it a suicide?" Mr. Scrivener frantically shook his head several times. The Reverend looked up at him. "Then it was murder."

"It might behoove you, sir, not to grin so widely," Miss Burrows remarked, refusing the Constable's arm. "Is it all so very humorous to you?" Her slender fingers rested anxiously on the brass knob to the study.

Mr. Edgewood raised his eyebrows. "Oh, you thought I was laughing at you? No, no, I was thinking of our earlier encounter with Lady Grace downstairs. Though I admit, I was thoroughly entertained by your joke about Mrs. Cox."

"I wasn't joking sir. I honestly didn't know who the Lady was."

"It was still marvelous. I'm—"

"The Constable, I know."

"Please call me Robert," he replied kindly.

"Robert?"

"Yes, Robert, or Mr. Edgewood if you must."

"Mr. Edgewood, then. We've only just become acquainted."

"And you are, Miss Burrows, was it?"

"Yes."

"And what is your first name?"

"My first name?"

"Yes."

"Frances."

"Frances?"

"Yes."

"Fanny?"

"Absolutely not!"

"I like Fanny," he grinned.

"Mr. Edgewood, I insist you call me Miss Burrows, or if you must, Miss Frances."

"If you insist… Miss Burrows. There's the study on the left. Are you ready?"

"You act like I've never done this before, Mr. Edgewood."

"Why, of course you have!" Mr. Edgewood assured her. "But in the privacy of your home with your father's supervision."

"I can do it," she mumbled, turning the doorknob. He offered her a handkerchief, "For the smell, Miss Burrows." She nodded in thanks, crouching to examine the state of the body and position of the gun.

"Clearly, it was an accidental misfire," he tested, gesturing to the wound in his skull. She folded her arms.

"Really! You really think it was an *accident* with a Lancaster pistol, Mr. Edgewood? I know better! The Lancaster is more reliable than the Beaumont-Adams and Colt Navy revolvers combined."

"I don't know many ladies who know so much about weaponry," Mr. Edgewood quipped.

"Nor I," she admitted. Mr. Edgewood clapped gleefully.

"Does your father let you shoot pistols too?"

"Once," she confessed. "Only once."

"Did you miss the target?"

"No. That's why I only needed to do it once." Her eyes twinkled, but her mind was otherwise engaged. "Was there no note, Mr. Edgewood?"

"Not from what Mrs. Cox claims," he replied cryptically. She pulled the handkerchief away from her face so that he might understand her speech. "You think she lied?"

"I think Mrs. Cox is the sort of woman who will do whatever necessary to keep her master's standing and honour. In short, I think it quite possible. She was the one to find him, after all."

Miss Burrows anxiously rubbed her hands. "And the servants were gone?"

"Yes. They had retired for the evening."

"He had no enemies?"

"None that Mrs. Cox would admit to."

"And vices?"

"Gambling."

She surveyed the room again. "That's strange," she said suddenly, her eyes stopping at the desk. "Look at that candle."

"What about it?"

"There are no wax drippings. Don't you find that odd?"

"They could have recently replaced the candle," he said dismissively.

"Who would be in here to replace it? Why would they? I find it hard to believe Mrs. Cox came in to do it."

"Your observation is irrelevant."

"Excuse me," she retorted. "You think my observations are irrelevant? Why? Because I'm a woman?"

"No, because I'm the Constable. And a Constable has to sort out what is useful and what is extemporaneous. A candle has no importance in an investigation like this. Surely you realize that. You are here as my assistant. You'd be good to remember it."

No amount of rouge could conceal the wear about her eyes. She hadn't slept well the previous night. Miss Mortimer knocked once outside before entering. "Sir Thomas has arrived, my Lady. Should I have him wait downstairs?"

The Lady licked her lips. "You may send him up, Ruth."

"My Lady, you are not yet fully dressed," Miss Mortimer taunted. "Perhaps I shall divert him with a story."

"Don't you dare tell him anything," she threatened. "Don't forget it's solely through my generosity you've been allowed to stay on." Miss Mortimer bowed her head. "I'm ever so grateful my Lady. As it is written, 'those who show mercy will be given it.'" Lady Grace looked over her shoulder at her. "Have I need of mercy, Ruth?" Miss Mortimer silently brushed her Lady's golden curls. Lady Grace admired herself in the mirror. "Isn't grief wonderful for a woman's figure?"

Ruth nodded in agreement. "Your Ladyship's figure is divine."

"That's what they tell me," she giggled. "I'm happy to say I still have many suitors, and will marry again soon. This time I hope he will not be so old. I have a feeling he won't be." Ruth knew whom she had in mind. "And what of Isaac, Ma'am?"

Lady Grace tilted her head. "Isaac? Oh, I haven't thought of that."

Miss Mortimer grabbed the brush handle tighter. "Maybe he should come home," she said softly.

"Why? He's not *my* son. Nor my late husband's for that matter. He's the brother of my Lord's bastard."

This particularly intrigued Miss Mortimer. "Where's the brother then?"

"Dead. He and the whore mother."

"I never knew that story," the cook remarked, a shadow passing over her face.

"Why would you know anything," the Lady retorted. "You know, he waited until after we were married to even tell me the child existed. Can you believe it? It was just thrust upon me he had taken the child in. For what purpose? He could have as easily got rid of it. Sent him to an orphanage."

Miss Mortimer choked. "So sorry my Lady. The air is so dry in here."

"Don't concern yourself with the boy, Ruth," Lady Grace remarked. "I know you care about him, seeing as you have watched him grow up. But he's nothing to me or to this family."

"I think he's a delightful boy, my Lady," she replied meekly. "He's very handsome."

"You would say that, you love children. Why don't you go and have one on your own, eh?"

"Perhaps one day, Ma'am. But, if you would forgive me for saying, I think the boy would be pleasant company. He'd bring some life into these walls again."

"I'd rather not. His ruckus always gives me a horrible headache."

"Leave him to me, my Lady! I'll keep him from being a nuisance."

"Let me make myself clear: that bastard is not coming here ever again. Now fetch me breakfast, Ruth, and send the gentlemen up. He's been left wanting for far too long."

"Waiting for you certainly does work up the appetite," Sir Thomas crooned. "That black dress is ravishing…. It'll be more ravishing when I see what is beneath it."

"No," she hissed. "Not now! Do you know why I sent for you?"

"Because it's Thursday morning, my sweet. And on Thursday mornings, we—"

"How can you even speak like that? As if nothing has happened?"

"Nothing has happened, except that your circumstances," he paused to touch her corset, "have changed. Don't you think it's time to 'hang up the ladle,' Grace? You've kept me waiting long enough," he whispered.

"Why so pale, my love? Surprised your bumbling oaf of a husband finally did himself in?"

"Is that what you are calling this!" She retrieved a letter from her corset and shoved it angrily into his hands. "Mrs. Cox gave it to me this morning."

The gentleman glanced at the contents, smirking. He then tossed it into the air, letting the letter float aimlessly to the ground. "We both knew there would be no other resolution. Why act so weak and pitiful? Save it for the constable. Everything is going better than we hoped. We can finally marry within the year."

"We will not." The gentleman's face reddened, his lips retreating into a scowl. For those who may not know, Sir Thomas Pryce was once the Master's most treasured companion. The pair was incredibly fond of playing cards. It should be noted that Sir Thomas always knew when to fold. Lord Walter did not.

"Scared off by a suicide are you? We have more pressing matters to attend to, like money for instance."

"There's no money left, Thomas. There's barely anything left for Isaac, and all of that is in a trust until he comes of age. Can't you see what is happening? Green Brier will fall into disrepair. You know what I must do."

"Are you completely mad," he yelled. "How deep into this are you? Your coward of a husband told me he'd pay me with double the interest! He told me he would pay!" He thrust his fist into the wall. "Damn him!"

Her jade green eyes widened. "You never told me he owed you money."

"You had no reason to know," he growled.

"'So is that why ... you and I —"

"Absolutely not," he replied, caressing her hair. "I am also in need of a pretty wife."

"You disgust me."

"I didn't kill him, Grace."

"Why wouldn't you, Thomas?" she said in a hoarse whisper.

"I wasn't even there," he whispered in her ear. She struck his chest violently.

"You were his friend and you stood there and watched him gamble away his entire fortune!"

"And you were his unfaithful *wife*," he snapped. "I told you, I wasn't even there that night."

"Then where were you?"

"London."

"Business?"

"Of sorts." He smirked.

"I see. Who is she?"

He kissed her forehead. "Nobody of consequence."

"I need to know, Thomas."

"My dear, you don't need to know anything. I hear Miss Mortimer coming up now. Since it's too late for anything *else*," he remarked while dressing again, "I beg your leave. I have a prior engagement."

"In London," she croaked.

"No, my Lady, in Surrey. Business of sorts." There was a knock outside her room. Sir Thomas excused himself, the cook curtseying as he passed.

"I guess he didn't want breakfast, Ma'am?"

Lady Grace swallowed, picking up the letter from the floor. She wasn't about to be bested by a man who ruined her family's reputation. She could accept his gambling, but not other affairs. What a fool he made of her! "Ruth, send for Mr. Edgewood. My husband had no accident. Sir Thomas killed him."

"Lady Grace," Mr. Edgewood said, bowing, "It's an honour to see you again." She shot a sideways glance at Miss Burrows. "I hope you don't mind," Mr. Edgewood added quickly, "I felt that Miss Burrows might be of assistance."

"I don't see why," her Ladyship remarked, "She has already taken his body."

"If you please my Lady," Miss Burrows said softly, "I wish to be of service."

The Mistress ignored her. "My dear Lady Grace," Mr. Edgewood remarked, taking her hand, "You look as lovely as ever. Black becomes you." The Lady stroked her hair impishly. "Your letter prompted us to come straightaway. Your accusations in your letter about Sir Thomas are . . . serious. This morning we took the liberty of breakfasting with your housekeeper, Mrs. Cox. It appears that she failed to mention a letter she discovered the night of the accident . . . I should inform your Ladyship that this new evidence may or may not support your theory. We were told Mrs. Cox placed this letter into your possession, and that the parchment suggests your husband's death to be suicide rather than murder. I would be able to confirm more if I were to see it myself."

"For all I know this is a forgery," she said defensively, offering the letter. Mr. Edgewood examined it carefully, and then passed it to Miss Burrows. She squinted at the letter, scrutinizing every word. "Is it in his hand?"

Lady Grace pouted. "I'm a very busy woman. I cared nothing of his business practices."

"You probably regret that now, I daresay." Mr. Edgewood gave her a sympathetic smile. She snorted in contempt. Her eyes were much duller than he had remembered.

"What makes you think Sir Thomas Pryce is responsible?" Miss Burrows asked hesitantly.

Lady Grace averted her eyes. "My husband owed him one thousand pounds. I don't need your pitiful looks girl! I knew my husband had debts, and a great deal many. However, I didn't know he was so indebted to Sir Thomas. They've been friends for fifteen years at least. I suppose I was blinded by something and failed to see what would happen."

Mr. Edgewood nodded. "Your cook told us of your affection for Sir Thomas. That's why we found the accusation rather unusual." She wiped her red-rimmed eyes. "He had more than enough motive. Don't you see that, Mr. Edgewood?"

"I see this case gets more and more peculiar as it goes on," he conceded. "First, it was accident rumored suicide and now it is a full-scale murder investigation." Mr. Edgewood handed her back the letter.

"Is it a forgery, Mr. Edgewood? Tell me plainly." Mr. Edgewood ruffled his hair again, attempting to recall the scene. Something about his recollections struck him odd, though he could not quite explain what.

"Mr. Edgewood," Miss Burrows interrupted. "The candle! Had Sir Walter written this letter in his hand, he would have used candlelight that evening. And there were no wax drippings, thus the letter could not have been written in the study. Why would Sir Walter write a letter elsewhere and then put it on the desk?"

"He must not have written it," they said together. "Then it was Sir Thomas," Lady Grace exclaimed.

"Maybe," Mr. Edgewood said slowly, "Maybe not."

Mr. Edgewood and Miss Burrows had been strolling together down the road in silence. A passerby might imagine this young couple enjoying an afternoon stroll together amidst the beautiful seaside, their minds on romance and poetry. In truth, the two were discussing the grisly details of a murder.

"Thank you for allowing me to accompany you on the case today, Mr. Edgewood."

"The pleasure was mine, Miss Burrows." He stopped a moment to face her directly. "I have a confession to make to you. When I first met you, I thought your presence was amusing. Yet you've continually surprised me with your cunning and gusto. You play the part of a gentle, docile creature, but beneath that lies a much more intriguing woman. A woman I should like to get to know very much." Miss Burrows carefully considered his admission, but did not soften toward him.

"I hope in the future you won't dismiss me so readily," she replied. "It was I who pointed out the candle to begin with. And if you recall, you were the one who said my observation was irrelevant."

"And I was wrong, Miss Burrows. You have been more of an asset to me than I realized. I think we work splendidly together. You were particularly on par with extracting that letter from Mrs. Cox. I wouldn't have been nearly as successful."

"I knew that frightening her with arrest would be effective," she blushed. "Though I'm a bit ashamed of having done so."

"It was spectacular, Fanny."

"Sir!"

"Miss Burrows," he corrected himself.

"It's a strange case, isn't it?" she asked, changing the subject.

He nodded in agreement. "Strange indeed. Stranger by the minute, I daresay."

Miss Burrows paused thoughtfully. "Do you believe Sir Thomas really committed it?"

"I'm not sure. Miss Mortimer seemed to have other ideas about it."

Miss Mortimer seems to have a lot of ideas," she observed. "The whole ordeal perplexes me. Sir Thomas and Sir Walter were close friends for many years. Her Ladyship and Sir Thomas possessed strong rapport. Why suddenly accuse him? For all we know, Sir Walter owed more to someone else of even more despicable character. I fear something is amiss."

Mr. Edgewood ruffled his hair. "That's just it: the only person with keys to enter the door was Mrs. Cox. I don't see her motive for killing him. But that gaping door suggests that either someone had the key—"

"Or someone let him in."

"Thus the killer must have been someone Sir Walter knew well. Someone he was comfortable allowing inside his study. His wife was away in Southampton. Though there are no witnesses to prove it."

"And where was Sir Thomas?" she inquired.

"I don't know," Mr. Edgewood replied. "But I suspect that Lady Grace and Sir Thomas are involved."

She looked at him skeptically. "Do you mean...*together*?"

He confirmed it. She scoffed. "But what leads you to believe that they—"

Mr. Edgewood shook his head. "She was far too defensive, Miss Burrows."

She was not convinced. "Perhaps Sir Thomas was elsewhere that evening."

"I've asked about town. They say he frequents London often, the northeast district to be precise."

"Opium dens?"

"No, the whorehouses." She grimaced. "Excuse me, Miss Burrows, I forgot myself. But that's what I was told."

"If you're right, he could not have had enough time to come back and kill Sir Walter either. Do you think she knew this?"

"Well, how would you feel if you were her?"

"Truthfully, Mr. Edgewood . . . *her* I will never be."

"Thank God for it. But really, what's a woman to do in her position?"

"I suppose some women might want revenge."

"Accusing a man of murder is pretty vengeful," he hinted. "But it still doesn't answer our big question. You know, I've been thinking about our mysteriously missing Mr. Scrivener. After sending for the Constable, he mysteriously disappears. Think it a coincidence?"

"Reverend, I must confess," Mr. Scrivener remarked, closing the Bible. "I've never understood the Book of Ruth."

The Reverend beamed, stoking the fireplace. "It is a story of love, honour, and faithfulness. A widow who follows her mother-in-law wherever she goes. She is tested and the Lord rewards her. She marries her husband's relative, and through her comes a legacy of salvation." Mr. Scrivener stared at the flames.

"It must have been difficult. Traveling to a strange land for the sake of family." The Reverend smiled kindly. "Family is the strongest bond there is, particularly a mother and child. Or in this case, mother-in-law." The fire crackled loudly in the hearth. "Any particular reason for asking, Charles?"

"It reminded me of a girl I know," Mr. Scrivener replied. "Her name is Ruth too."

"Ah, your sweetheart, I suppose?" Reverend Knightley chuckled cheerfully.

"I would wish it were so. Alas Reverend, she's not mine." The Reverend paused to see if the man would continue. "I know I've never mentioned her before. She's the cook at Green Brier. The Master never *appreciated* her the way I did. Yet the Master's son was quite fond of her. She always brought him cookies, and was quite gentle with the little chap.

Then Sir Walter sent him away, and there was no one for her to make cookies for...." His voice trailed off. The Reverend sensed there was more.

"I've read that the investigation into Sir Walter's death continues. They're calling it murder now, yet they have no suspects."

"No plausible ones anyways," Mr. Scrivener corrected. "Sir Thomas is their best lead."

"Greed is one of the strongest motivators for murder, Mr. Scrivener. Money and power, that is what it all comes down to."

"Love is also powerful reason."

"Love as a reason to kill?"

"Well," Mr. Scrivener reasoned, "A soldier loves his country, his Queen, his God—he kills for what he believes."

"That is not murder."

"But is it possible, Reverend," Mr. Scrivener asked earnestly, "that a person might kill for selfless reasons? To kill for love?"

"It's a tangled web," the Reverend professed. "A tempting trap. People do kill for love, for honour, revenge...and in everything you read, it ends badly. You see it in the Bible, and in the greatest literature of the world—the bad must be punished, the good rewarded."

"Can a good person ever do something bad for a good reason?"

"Yes. But it doesn't change the fact it was murder."

"Loyalty is a virtue, Reverend. The truth is she wasn't happy. All the servants knew it. And we all knew where it went to. The Lady had vices too, and secrets. I have secrets too, Reverend. Lady Grace was not in Southampton the night of the murder."

"Let me in," a man roared from outside the door. "There's no time to waste!"

The door opened. "Are you Miss Burrows?" the tall gentleman asked. She nodded. "Where's the Constable from London?"

"Mr. Edgewood's not here. To whom am I speaking?"

"Charles Scrivener, the footman of –"

"Mr. Scrivener," she exclaimed. "You're the one we've been looking for!"

"So the secret has been discovered then!"

Miss Burrows raised her eyebrows. "I don't know what you mean."

"Where is the boy, Miss Burrows?" he demanded. "Where's Isaac!"

"He came home yesterday," she said blankly. Mr. Scrivener paused. "And where is she?"

"Her Ladyship has gone missing. Mrs. Cox saw her walking near the cliffs early this morning, and she hasn't been seen since. There's suspicion of suicide!" Miss Burrows found the idea unfathomable. "Why would she?" she thought. "Unless…"

The door burst open. "Mr. Scrivener," Miss Mortimer screeched. "I've been looking for you!"

"I know you have Ruth."

"You didn't," Miss Mortimer whispered desperately. "Charlie, you didn't." His solemn expression caused her to run outside. A tawny-haired boy was sitting patiently in the cart. Miss Mortimer saw the approaching carriage cresting the hill.

"Stop right there," Constable Chadwick yelled. "In the name of the law! There! Hold her there!"

"Miss Burrows," Mr. Edgewood bellowed from inside the carriage. Constable Chadwick rushed out and positioned himself between Miss Mortimer and the boy. "You're coming with us, Ruth!" he exclaimed, grabbing her arm roughly. The cook yelped in pain from his grip.

"You might want to hear what she has to say first, sir," Mr. Edgewood remarked to the Constable.

"I didn't have to bring you, Mr. Edgewood," the Constable said through gritted teeth. ""I'm here because the Chief sent for me, since you couldn't get the job done. You couldn't even complete your first investigation! I guess you don't have the stomach for it."

Miss Mortimer screamed at the footman, "You called the coppers! You did this!"

"I had no choice Ruth," Mr. Scrivener pleaded. "You know I didn't. I tried to hide it. I went to the Reverend and stayed silent hoping you'd get away. That you might finally have him back." Constable Chadwick threw her into the carriage, despite protests from Mr. Scrivener and the boy.

"Is it necessary to traumatize the boy," Mr. Edgewood asked him. "Have some common decency."

"The Chief was right about you," Chadwick spat. "You officers…always touting off about honour and what's right. You think what she did was right? Knocking off a gentleman? Her employer, no less?"

"She had a reason, sir. Maybe not the right reason." Chadwick grunted. "No reason that establishes her innocence."

The boy whimpered. Mr. Edgewood noticed Miss Burrows' perplexed expression. "Consider the evidence, Miss Burrows: the letter pleading for Isaac to return home. The lack of wax drippings, which suggested the suicide note as a forgery. And then Miss Mortimer, who suggested something amiss with Lord Sir Charles, then her Ladyship, and even Sir Thomas, anything to distract from the truth."

Miss Burrows finally understood. "Isaac is your *son?*"

Miss Mortimer spoke emptily through the carriage window. "Sir Walter is his father. I was sixteen when Isaac was born. Then he stole my son from me to raise as his own. When he decided to send Isaac away to school, I begged the Master to keep him with me. He refused. He often left his study unlocked in the evenings when I brought him tea. I knew where he kept the gun. So I wrote the letter, grabbed the gun, and shot him straight in the head. God have mercy, I shot him."

"You have to understand why she did it," Mr. Scrivener interjected. "It wasn't for money or power. It was for Isaac."

The boy in the cart began to cry louder. "Please, let me take my boy," she begged.

"You can't take him with you," Constable Chadwick replied gruffly. "You're no mother to him. You are nuthin' but a murderer."

"Mr. Edgewood please," she bawled. "Don't let them take Isaac. What will happen to my boy?"

Mr. Scrivener ran up to kiss her hand through the bars. "I'll take Isaac," he soothed. "I'll make sure he's well cared for."

"I'm going to hang," she announced to them. "For protecting my son."

"You'll hang for murder," Constable Chadwick reminded her. "There's a difference."

"Chadwick," Mr. Edgewood began, but his voice left him. The Constable climbed into the carriage, signaling for the coachman to drive on. Miss Mortimer did not stop screaming or crying for an instant, her voice echoing over the cliffs and across the ocean to any who might hear a mother's plea. "I've sacrificed everything for you, Isaac," she screamed from a distance. The boy continued sniveling, clutching a handkerchief. Mr. Scrivener could hardly look at the departing carriage.

He glanced up at the Constable. "Is there a chance she may be pardoned, sir?"

Mr. Edgewood exhaled deeply, ruffling his hair. "I doubt it, Mr. Scrivener."

Miss Burrows took the boy's frail hand. "Would you like to come inside for some cookies, Isaac?"

"No Ma'am," he sniveled. "I think I should like to go home to Green Brier."

She searched Mr. Edgewood's eyes. "Who will care for the boy now?"

"I'll take the boy to Mrs. Cox. She'll know what to do," Mr. Scrivener assured her, climbing into the cart.

"Do you think Mrs. Cox knew?"

Mr. Scrivener shrugged. "That Ruth's his mother? We may never know. But she'll do him right."

"That housekeeper is of 'sturdy stock,'" Mr. Edgewood said grimly.

"I'm sorry I never told you before, sir," the footman confessed. "I tried to act upon my conscience, albeit too late."

"We do our best," Mr. Edgewood replied, "No more, no less." The two respectfully shook hands.

And so the footman and Isaac, Sir Walter and his cook's bastard, rode off into a fading horizon an uncertain fate.

"Dry your tears, Miss Burrows," Mr. Edgewood said gently. "It'll be all right."

"I never expected this," she sniffed, "I thought it'd be a real black-heart, a villain. Not her."

"Justice has been served this day," he contemplated. "Well... England's sort of justice."

Miss Burrows sensed his uneasiness about Constable Chadwick and his methods. "You tried, Mr. Edgewood," she remarked. "That's more than some can say." She wiped her misty eyes. Despite the vision of this beautiful woman in all her vulnerability, Mr. Edgewood considered instead how much assistance she might be to him in the future. He had need of her special qualities.

"Perhaps we should go inside and have a cup of tea," he said softly.

"Tea," she huffed. "At a time like this?"

"Tea solves a lot of troubles, Fanny."

"Miss Burrows!" she corrected, wagging her finger at him.

The Constable winked, revealing his playful dimple.

"As for tea," the woman answered pensively. "I think not, Mr. Edgewood. Today I feel I shall remain unsatisfied."

2016

Photo Smarts

Helen Hufford

"A picture is worth a thousand words." – Napoleon Bonaparte
"One picture is worth 1,000 denials." – Ronald Reagan

"The game this afternoon?" Carly asked wide-eyed, as she nibbled on her lower lip.

"That's right. I need someone to cover it," Ginny Kane replied. "Come on, Carly. Don't let me down." Ginny touched her shoulder assuredly.

"But I didn't bring my camera to school today," Carly answered sulkily.

"Use mine," her teacher grinned as she handed her the case." Now, scoot and don't be late. The game starts at four. I'll ask Mrs. Candiotti to let you out of detention early." Ginny laughed as she walked out the door.

Carly watched the game from the bleachers. She followed her friend, Katie, with her eyes, camera poised for an action shot. Just as Katie was rising to take a shot from behind the line, Carly was prepared to take a shot herself. Swoosh! Three points. St. Anne Academy had won! Carly was confident that this one would be featured in the online school newspaper. Photojournalism usually involved more writing than Carly cared to think about, but sometimes a little luck at being in the right place at the right time could help out. Take for instance this afternoon. This was the first chance Carly had at impressing her friends, parents, and teacher with her photography. Although she grudgingly accepted the assignment from Mrs. Kane, she did want to see her byline and photograph on the school website. Katie would be really happy too. Carly knew Katie was trying to land an athletic scholarship, and coaches from colleges she was interested in would be impressed. Satisfied with the work she had done, Carly smiled to herself and sighed softly.

Immediately after the game, Carly joined her friends at the Red Robin across the street from the gym. She waited in line for only a minute when Emma wedged her way through the crowd and poked Carly in the ribs.

"Follow me," she mouthed, not bothering to compete with the background music, waitresses and a huge robin mascot singing "Happy Birthday" to an eight-year-old, and the chatter from the rest of the basketball game spectators who were pouring through the double doors of the restaurant.

"Joe and I left one minute before the end of game to get this table," Emma explained as she took a sideways glance at her newest boyfriend, a lean and lanky forward in his fourth year at St. Ignatius High School.

"Too bad. You missed the best part. Katie scored during the last fifteen seconds of the game. It was fantastic," Lauren commented. "It was totally out of the blue."

"Carly, where were you?" Emma asked, cocking her head to the side.

"Yeah. Where were you? I was in the gym sitting on the right side, under the cross country championship banner, with Jacob, where we were all supposed to meet, but we didn't see you there," Lauren said as she reached for a nacho chip and absent-mindedly double dipped.

"I was taking pictures from the other side of the gym. I'm glad Mrs. Kane asked me to help out this afternoon in spite of the fact that it kept me from sitting with you guys, and I had to use her camera," Carly explained to her friends. She sipped her chocolate malt milkshake, the reward she allowed herself for a job well done, before pulling the camera out of her handbag and passing it around the table.

"Awesome. Let me see the pictures." Lauren implored as she brushed the crumbs from her fingertips onto the napkin on her lap.

"Pretty impressive work. Katie will be so happy you took this picture of her winning shot," Lauren crossed her legs, and reached for another nacho.

"Look. You and I are in the background of this shot, Emma" Joe pointed out, passing the camera back.

Sam sat down next to her brother, Jacob, just as the camera was again handed around the table. Typically a high scoring forward center for St. Anne's, Sam broke her arm in a pick-up game in her neighborhood two days ago. The coach and her parents, who were grounding her this coming weekend, were furious with her for recklessly playing around when her team was counting on her.

"Lucky Katie," Sam stared blankly at the photos Carly had taken.

"We're in Katie's shot, too," Lauren pointed out to Jacob. "I can't believe I really look like that when I laugh."

"Oh, you do" Emma confirmed. "I swear you do."

"Thanks for being so honest" Lauren replied, feeling the vibration of her cell phone in her pocket.

"What are friends for?" quipped Emma, crinkling her eyes and nose.

"I'm the only person not in a picture from the game!" complained Sam, "It seems weird."

"Say cheese" Lauren, who happened to be holding the camera, snapped a candid shot of Sam who made a funny face on cue. "Now you have nothing to complain about."

The camera circled around the table once more. Lauren excused herself to check her text messages in private, a habit she acquired from attending a school for girls. She returned a few minutes later, a more subdued Lauren.

"You guys. I need to return that camera to Mrs. Kane" Carly forced a tight-lipped smile. "I'm going to try to catch a ride home with Anna over there," she said. She quickly made her way across the restaurant and then hurried back to grab her backpack, leave money for the check, and pick up Mrs. Kane's camera.

In the midst of the now half-full Red Robin, the rest of the group settled up the bill and disbanded.

The next day at 2:25 pm, Ginny had the front office page Carly Beaumont to come down before leaving the school building.

"Carly, I expected you to return my camera this morning," Ginny raised her eyebrows. Carly, who had been a star on the hockey field last fall, underwent knee surgery during the winter break. She missed so many classes this semester that Ginny was worried about her academically. Ginny, who wanted to see Carly earn a good grade and enjoy the class, assigned the basketball game to her because she knew that Carly had a strong interest in sports.

"I'm sorry" Carly replied. She had stored it in her locker first thing that morning and really could not find the time to run it back to the photojournalism room during the fifteen minute break the students were allotted. "I got some great pictures. Hope you like them." Carly placed the camera in Mrs. Kane's outstretched hands and fled.

Later that evening, Ginny was expected to take photographs at the new archbishop's reception at St. Anne Academy. She arrived in the nick of time with her camera in hand. A photographer from Galeone was also scheduled to attend the event, but Ginny was accustomed to cover virtually all of the school events to snap a variety of photographs for the yearbook and other school publications. On this March evening, as the archbishop stepped into the foyer of the school building, he was warmly greeted by the principal and vice-principals of the school.

"Good evening, Your Excellency," the sisters said, each in turn.

"So pleased to meet you," he replied graciously.

Ginny selected the best vantage point while introductions ensued. Snap. Snap. After a few candid shots she walked over to a secluded corner of the Music Hall to double check her camera. When she snapped the pictures, she was aware of an unusual icon hovering in the left corner of the viewfinder that she had never seen before. Blast it! The memory card was missing. Thank goodness a professional photographer had just arrived. Ginny frowned and then pulled out her cell phone and called home.

The home phone was answered promptly, for a change.

"Hi, Katelyn, I have a question for you. Were you checking the pictures on my school camera right after school today?" Ginny asked, tapping her foot all the while.

"No, Mom, why?" her daughter replied. Ginny told her she was just wondering. Katelyn, a sophomore at St. Anne's, who was used to having a mother with a reputation as the school sleuth, knew better than to press her for more information.

"I know our paths might have crossed for a few minutes right after school, but I've been at dance class helping Miss Lisa with the kindergarteners for most of the afternoon. Now I'm working on my chemistry homework. Oh, yes, I also took Shadow for a walk and fed him. Dad brought Chinese carry-out. When will you be home?" Katelyn added.

"I'll be home soon." Ginny responded as she glanced around the Music Hall, content that Galeone had everything under control.

On Friday morning, Ginny wanted to hurry to school after leading her boot camp aerobics session at the Western YMCA from 6:00-6:50 am, a favorite among many of the working women in Catonsville. However, instead, she maintained her cool as she let her sixteen-year-old daughter drive her there. Ginny, known for her high energy level and abundant enthusiasm, tried to live up to the popular image she projected, and nearly always succeeded. She enjoyed her part-time teaching job at St. Anne Academy more than her part-time job as a reporter for the Catonsville Times, even though it sometimes led to a migraine. She was working on practicing patience, so she took the morning drive with Katelyn as an opportunity to strengthen her endurance.

The aroma of cinnamon buns filled the hallway emanating from the Rose Room where the Scholar's Breakfast for the newly inducted honor society members was underway. Ginny strolled into the Rose Room, centrally located in the school and decorated in a Victorian style featuring pictures of various types of roses on every wall, to grab a cup of coffee and a donut before heading upstairs to the photojournalism classroom. Shirley Candiotti stood next to the coffee dispenser, pouring multiple creamers into her coffee mug. Ginny walked over to where she was standing and reached for a packet of sugar.

"Good morning. I need to talk to you privately. Do you have a minute?" Ginny stirred her coffee and glanced around the room.

"Sure. Meet me in my office right after the beginning of first block. You're off then, aren't you?" Ginny nodded, and Shirley picked up her plate of goodies and headed out the door.

Halfway through the first block, Ginny sunk into the chair facing Shirley and set her second cup of coffee and donut on the table by her side. Shirley left the door ajar, but shut it enough for a private conversation with Ginny, before she slid into the chair next to her.

"Someone stole the memory card from my camera – the school camera" Ginny blurted out.

"Wait. Aren't I usually asking for your help in tracking down the culprits around here?" Mrs. Candiotti, the vice-principal in charge of discipline, asked. Over the years that Ginny had been employed at St. Anne Academy, she had impressed the administration with her ability to identify the delinquents in several incidents that quite frankly had left them baffled. Last year, disturbing graffiti in the girl's gym locker room and in a few of the lavatories proved to be a difficult case to solve. With her understanding of the nature of adolescents, and a little luck, Kane discovered the identity of the guilty party, an emotionally charged student struggling with the break-up of her parents' marriage. During the previous year, Ginny came to Shirley's aid twice. First, in the fall, when Daphne Zenith was livid because her Bath & Body Works hand sanitizers were stolen from her classroom, Ginny tracked down the thief and extracted a confession. Then, she demonstrated her prowess again that year when she uncovered the exploits of a handful of seniors who had cut classes for weeks during the spring. In addition to her strong intuition and powers of observation, Ginny's natural warmth and upbeat personality made her a likely confidante for the girls. Consequently, she was often privy to information that eluded others from her generation.

Shirley sipped her coffee tentatively and placed her index finger on her temple. "Tell me about it." She was ready to listen.

"Carly Beaumont used the camera to take pictures at the basketball play-off on Wednesday. She returned it to me yesterday afternoon, at the end of the school day. I had to call her down to the front office to get it. After I took a few pictures at the archbishop's reception last night, I discovered that the memory card was missing," Ginny relayed the bad news as concisely as possible. "We've lost all of the pictures from the basketball game," Ginny grimaced and stuffed a piece of donut into her mouth.

"Well, this is the second theft I've heard of this week." Shirley confided. "Heather told me she thinks a test was taken from the top drawer of her desk." She broke another donut in two and recalled the events of last year's bout of kleptomania in the school. "I don't know what to think. Last year, we were all convinced that the worst was over when Jill Moran withdrew from school in the spring. The string of thefts throughout the school suddenly stopped. Now it's happening all over again. This déjà vu is unnerving."

"I doubt that the two events are related," offered Ginny. "Rumors of a rise in cheating on tests have been circulating recently, but—."

A rap on the door interrupted their conversation.

"Mrs. Candiotti, may I come in?" Giselle Montague, an English teacher from the third floor, asked.

"Yes, Giselle," Mrs. Candiotti approached the door to respond to the second emergency of the day. Lately, she always seemed to have an endless list of crises at her door.

"The cell phones of Lauren Cole and Maura Wilson both went off in the middle of our Holocaust class. Here they are." Giselle placed the phones on the desk of the disciplinarian.

"OK." Shirley browsed her list of cell phone violators, and sure enough, this was Lauren's second offense. "It looks like she's up for in-school suspension. I'll see them both at the end of the day."

Ginny left Shirley Candiotti's office and entered the photojournalism classroom where a dozen juniors and seniors were gathered around computers, ready to edit articles and lay out the next online edition of the school newspaper.

"Mrs. Kane, we're finished with the article about Mr. Miller's presentation from the assembly two weeks ago. Would you like to take a look at it?" Emma called out from the back of the room.

"Sure." Ginny skimmed through the article. "Great job! We're going to feature it. I knew I could count on you." Ginny pumped Emma up with her contagious enthusiasm.

"Do you think we have enough room to include this 2001 yearbook picture of his daughter?" Anna asked.

"Yes, that's a terrific idea," Ginny responded. She was wondering how they would fill in the gap now that the pictures from the basketball game were missing. She wanted to balance the article on Mr. Miller's presentation on date rape and violence with something positive like the winning game. Ginny also wanted to see Carly's work recovered. Carly had an opportunity to shine, and Ginny did not want to see her lose her chance. She was disappointed that Carly had not been more careful with the camera. If only the memory card would turn up undamaged.

"We were all stunned by Mr. Miller's presentation," Anna said as she located the picture of Sophie Miller. "How are we going the get this photo on the website? It wasn't taken with a digital camera back then."

"We'll scan it in, Anna. I'll show you how." Ginny replied. Placing the yearbook on the scanner, Ginny recalled seeing Sophie Miller in the hallways of St. Anne's years ago. Sophie had not been in any of her classes, but she was just like the girls Ginny taught, full of promise and high spirits. Happy one day, stressed out the next. Sophie's father had not been back to his daughter's alma mater in eleven years, since the day of Sophie's graduation ceremony. Giselle Montague had invited him to talk to the seniors about the dangers of date rape and violence. In his PowerPoint presentation, he displayed beautiful pictures of his daughter, some that were taken right at St. Anne Academy. Sophie had just graduated from Villanova, seven years ago, when a boyfriend she had met working in a restaurant in Philadelphia murdered her. He had stabbed her fifty-five times. During the past few years, Mr. Miller had started speaking to teenage girls about the warning signs of a potentially violent boyfriend. Sophie's boyfriend had been a controlling guy who tried to separate Sophie from her friends. He wanted to know where Sophie was and kept tabs on her by frequently texting and calling her on her cell phone. One of the last text messages Sophie sent to a friend raised the question that still haunts her family. Why did her boyfriend insist on control over her comings and goings? Sophie had decided to break up with him, and she made the mistake of doing it in person. Mr. Miller advised the seniors to break up with controlling boyfriends over the phone and then to immediately surround themselves with friends and family.

"I had a boyfriend who was too controlling for me last year," Emma said. "When he would text me, he even asked me to send photos of where I was at. He acted like he didn't trust me, and like I wasn't good enough for him. But he always called me every day and wanted to talk. I'm so glad Ethan decided to go to college in another state and that he's out of my life now. Once in a while he makes a comment on Facebook, but I ignore it."

During the break time following second block Carly entered the classroom and plopped her backpack on the floor. She slid into a chair and started to log onto the computer.

Ginny walked over to where Carly was sitting and took a deep breath.

"Hi, Mrs. Kane," Carly looked up.

"Carly, the memory card that was in the camera I loaned you is missing," Ginny informed her coolly.

"You're kidding," Carly's mouth dropped. She pushed her chair away from the computer and stared at Ginny. With a puzzled look, Carly shook her head and moaned, "Tell me it isn't true."

"I'm sorry to say that it most definitely is true," Ginny assured her.

"I can't believe it." Carly was dumbfounded. "But this is just my luck. Nothing turns out right for me," she lamented.

"Tell me everything that happened the afternoon you took the pictures at the game," Ginny probed. She wished Carly would save the drama for another day. She was in no mood for it now.

"After the game I met my friends at the Red Robin across the street. I showed the pictures I took to all of them," Carly explained, as her furrowed brow and trembling lips displayed her anxiety. "I had a great shot of Katie scoring the winning points."

"Would you say that the camera was in plain sight the entire time that you and your friends were passing it around the table?" Ginny inquired.

"Yeah, I think so," Carly replied as she tried to recall exactly what had happened at Red Robin. "I mean we were looking at the pictures together."

"Did you leave the table at all while your friends were looking at the pictures?" Ginny focused on gathering the facts as she concealed her increasing annoyance with Carly's nonchalant handling of the camera.

"Well I had to arrange for a ride home, so I left the table to speak to someone who might be able to give me a ride," Carly remembered. "You did ask me to cover the basketball game at the last minute, and I had to make arrangements to get home," she added defensively.

"Do you think someone at your table might have taken the memory card?" Ginny pressed on.

Carly was reluctant to provide any information about her friends, but she did say, "Sam might have been jealous of the picture I took of Katie." The whole situation made her feel sick.

Later that day, Ginny was chewing on a celery stick when Heather Harrison walked into the faculty lunch room. Most of the teachers had returned to their classrooms, so Ginny and Heather were alone.

"Hi, how's it going?" Ginny put her celery down and wiped her mouth with her napkin.

"Can't complain too much," Heather replied and placed a stack of ungraded papers on the table. She opened the refrigerator freezer and filled her mug with ice.

"I heard that you're missing a test, and you think it might have been stolen," Ginny was determined to learn more about the incident that occurred in Heather's class.

"It looks suspicious, but I might have misplaced the test" Heather admitted. "When I was returning unit tests back to my first block class, I didn't have Erin O'Hara's with the set. She's one of my best students. She asked, 'Where is my test, Mrs. Harrison?' and I told her that I must have placed it with the other class's work. But the other class really hasn't been tested on that material yet."

"Where do you usually keep the tests?" asked Ginny.

"When I'm in a hurry, and to keep them in a convenient place, I usually place them in a handy desk drawer. But in light of the rumors I've heard lately, I'll start keeping them under lock and key," Heather looked down and poured iced tea into her mug. "I have looked everywhere for that test, Ginny, and I can't imagine where it is."

"Well, it looks like you will need a good alternative for your other section," Ginny glanced at her watch, realized she needed to meet a student in two minutes, and headed out the door. At least Heather can resolve her problem with another test, Ginny thought.

After Katelyn drove her home from school, Ginny relaxed for a few moments before checking her email messages. When she went into the family room to use the computer, Katelyn was already there, logged onto Facebook. Normally, her daughter would quickly switch to another site the moment she came near the computer, but Katelyn was busily inspecting photos and she didn't hear her mother enter the room.

"Anything new and interesting there?" Ginny inquired.

Katelyn smiled and said, "I was tagged in a few pictures. Would you like to take a look?"

"Sure would," Ginny looked over her shoulder and her eyes widened. Nice shot if I say so myself, she thought.

The next morning, Ginny's first photojournalism class started after break time. Some of the students had entered the classroom and were casually discussing their plans for spring vacation as they logged onto their computers. Giselle quietly walked across the room to Ginny.

"I'm here at your request," she almost whispered as she placed her tote bag by the desk.

"I knew I could count on you. Thanks for watching this class," Ginny replied. Ginny paced over to the doorway and waited to intercept one student in particular before class began.

As Lauren approached the door, Ginny caught her eyes and stated matter-of-factly, "Lauren, we need to talk in Mrs. Candiotti's office." They walked down the staircase in abject silence. Lauren's hands clutched the books she was carrying while Ginny deliberately quickened the pace behind her. A passerby stole a glance and then averted her eyes as Ginny and Lauren entered the disciplinarian's office. Mrs. Candiotti, who was sitting behind her desk sipping coffee, rose and closed the door.

"Lauren, Mrs. Kane has brought you to my office because a memory card is missing from a school camera, and we think you may be able to help up locate it." Shirley began.

"I heard Carly say that a memory card was missing," Lauren responded sullenly. "But I don't know anything about it."

Ginny looked squarely at Lauren, whose eyes darted towards the door. "Lauren, did you see the pictures Carly took at the basketball game?"

"Briefly. She was showing them to a lot of people at Red Robin right after the game." Lauren retorted. "Sam was really jealous of the picture of Katie. Maybe you should question her and leave me alone."

"Lauren, could you tell us what you remember about the pictures you saw?" asked Ginny.

"She took a bunch of pictures. Some were good and some weren't. What's your point? I don't have a photographic memory. Some of my friends were in the pictures. Maybe they didn't like the way they looked. Carly isn't the greatest photographer," Lauren stated as she flipped her hair over her shoulder. "I doubt that we really could've used the pictures on the school website anyway."

Ginny sat down at Shirley's computer and proceeded to log onto Facebook. She brought up a photo that her daughter Katelyn, her Facebook "friend," was tagged in.

"Lauren, I recognize this photo as one that I took myself at the Support the Troops service project at BWI Thurgood Marshall last week. A group of us were there to greet soldiers as they reentered the states. I didn't choose to place this particular photo on the school website, but here it is on Facebook, and you're in the picture, too. Front and center." Ginny glared at Lauren.

"Really, Mrs. Kane. I don't even know your daughter. Anyone in that picture could've placed that on Facebook. Someone else from our class must have uploaded the picture and tagged your daughter," Lauren argued.

"But the digital trail leads back to you, Lauren. You posted the picture and tagged Anna and Meg. You've been hanging around with them in photojournalism class. Maybe you weren't aware that Meg and Katelyn both run track and are pretty good friends. Meg tagged Katelyn in the photo. It's really not that hard to see that you did post the picture, and you found it on my memory card," Ginny claimed.

"Why did you take the memory card, Lauren?" Shirley interjected.

Tears were forming in the eyes of the senior.

"I had to prevent Carly from featuring the picture of Katie scoring at the basketball game," Lauren admitted. "Me and Jacob were in that picture together. Even though he is Sam's brother and I practically just met him, my boyfriend would never understand if he saw it online. If my jealous boyfriend ever saw that picture, he'd make my life miserable!" Lauren sobbed. "When I listened to Mr. Miller's story about his daughter, I realized that Ian was too controlling. He has spent so much time texting me. I can hardly stand it."

Mrs. Candiotti still had Lauren's cell phone in her desk because neither of her parents had picked it up yet. She took it out now and handed it to Lauren who brought up her list of missed calls.

"Just look at all of the text messages he sent today," Lauren cried. "He's driving me crazy." Evidently, Ian had been texting Lauren several times a day over the past few weeks.

"He has been making your life miserable," responded Ginny, handing Lauren a Kleenex tissue. "You need to get away from him, and we need the memory card back."

"I've tried, but it's not that easy," Lauren whimpered. Two months to the day, Lauren had met Ian during play practice at St. Ignatius. Although she had been flattered by his attention at first, more and more frequently she resented accounting for her whereabouts to him. Now that Mrs. Kane and Mrs. Candiotti were aware of the social pressure Lauren had been feeling, she felt the weight of it lift off her chest.

Ginny placed her arm around Lauren's shoulders and assured her, "Take it easy. Lauren."

Lauren dabbed her eyes with a tissue and sighed. She reached for her backpack and withdrew the memory card from it. She handed it to Ginny and looked down at the floor.

"Come on, let's see if we can crop that picture and use it with the basketball story." Ginny was optimistic. "You can help me with it."

"Really?" Lauren brightened up.

"It won't hurt to take a look and try," Ginny felt determined to salvage some part of the photo for Lauren, Carly, and Katie.

As she was packing up her tote bag at the end of the school day, Ginny heard footsteps outside her classroom door. Heather popped her head inside and smiled.

"The mystery has been solved," Heather danced around the room.

"Yeah, but I don't see why you're celebrating," Ginny raised her eyebrow, still dwelling on the events of the day.

"Erin, you know, the student who claimed I didn't give her test back to her, stopped by a few moments ago. She told me she had found her test in her folder. She knew I had been looking for it, and she didn't want me to worry about it. It seems that when she stopped by to make up a quiz right before class, the other day, I gave her test back to her before I handed them to the class. Neither one of us remembered it!" Heather was relieved.

Heather, oblivious to the memory card mystery, made Ginny laugh out loud.

"I'm glad you could solve that one on your own, Heather," Ginny smiled.

"It's such a relief to me. I'd hate to think that my students were rummaging through the drawers of my desk," Heather admitted.

"Well, chalk that one up to sleep deprivation," retorted Ginny, as she escorted Heather out, turned off the light, and locked the door of the photojournalism classroom.

Work cited:
"Picture Quotes." BrainyQuote.com. Xplore Inc, 2012, 11 April 2012.

2012

Where's the Canary?

Nicole Stout

S he knew what she had become, but had not felt worried until this point: a goomata, not simply a mistress, but a necessary part of life for a mobster. At 28, her life was just as she wanted it to be while she was growing up; she lived in a beautiful condo, drove a Cadillac, and spent her days alternating between hostessing at a local Italian restaurant owned by one of her boyfriend's associates, and shopping at The Mall at Short Hills, never once worrying about seeing a bill, much less paying one. Her lifestyle was completely funded by her sometimes-present boyfriend.

Thinking of Anthony was what brought about her current awful feelings. While she looked around at her lavish surroundings, she cursed Tony out loud.

"How dare he? How could he?"

She paced so furtively that her long-haired cat, usually full of energy, had given up any hope of receiving attention and now watched her with lazy eyes from the leather couch. Adriana wasn't sure what to do, and wasn't even sure she could ask anybody.

What had Adriana so concerned was that she hadn't heard a word from Anthony in three days; one or two days could be forgiven, it was the nature of having a boyfriend with a wife and family who was connected to the mafia. Three days was unheard of; her calls and texts to his private cell phone had gone unanswered, and he hadn't even popped in the restaurant or stopped by her place, a habit he had taken up when they first met.

"That's it Fido," she said to the cat, now nodding its head sleepily. "I have to do something."

What she decided to do was the one thing she promised herself she would never do again, not to mention that she had sworn an oath to Anthony as well.

"I'm off to see Mikey."

As Adriana sat in traffic on Route 3, heading to Mikey's office in Patterson, she reminisced about the relationship they once had, a silly fling in her mind, but something much more to Mikey, and certainly more to Anthony. She was young and foolish, renting a house for the summer on Long Beach Island. She and a few of her girlfriends (she couldn't even remember who anymore) had headed out for a night of dancing and drinking in Seaside Heights, home to Jersey's finest. The mere thought that she had ever entered the club Karma almost made her gag now. From across the room she spotted the buff and very handsome young man, who later came over with a Zima (a Zima, for God's sake!) and introduced himself as Mikey.

The two struck up a "friends with benefits" relationship that continued through the summer. Adriana wasn't looking for anything serious at the time, and was unaware that Mikey was. He tried his best to sweep her off her feet, planning nights out in Hoboken and romantic dinners in the city. While Adriana lived at home with her parents, Mikey lived in a gorgeous apartment in Englewood and when she questioned (as she often did) where he got all his money, as he never seemed to be at work, he shrugged her off without an answer. Finally, as the "benefits" aspect of the relationship fizzled and the two became actual friends, Mikey revealed that he was "connected."

"Connected like how?" Adriana asked naively.

"Jesus, Adriana, you *are* from Jersey aren't you? Connected like connected, like I have friends in high places who make things happen."

"HAHA! Like the mafia? You're involved with the Mafia?"

"Yeah, it that so hard to believe?"

"Kind of…you're like a dopey version of…I don't even know who to compare you to…but it's someone really dopey."

"Adriana, I'm not kidding. My father grew up with the DeCavalcantes, and he introduced me."

"So what, do ya kill people, shake them down, run a strip club? What's the deal?"

"Nah, none of that. I'm more on the legal side. That's why I'm takin' classes at Union County in Criminal Justice."

Adriana thought back to that conversation and the many others that followed. Eventually, the "benefits" of their friendship subsided and they rode the crest of actual friendship: camaraderie, laughs over dinner, and a comfort she hadn't found with a male since kindergarten. As she drove, she tried to construct something that would make sense, especially in the face of the arguments Mikey was bound to make.

She took a few deep breaths as she pulled up to the all- glass building that housed Mikey's office; he now passed himself off as a somewhat respectable detective. Adriana laughed as she thought of all the "help" he had building his business, only after he had managed to be rejected by the Sheriff's Department as well as several town police departments. She checked her makeup and hair in the mirror, took a few more deep breaths and vowed that she would approach the situation calmly and rationally.

"Where the fuck is he Mikey?" The sheer volume of Adriana's voice was matched by the force with which she stormed through the office, leaving two stunned secretaries and three slammed doors in her wake. "So much for being calm" she thought.

"Ad, calm down. What's going on?" Mikey questioned his clearly flustered friend.

"I know you know something. Where the hell is Tony? What's going on?"

"Ad, I swear, I have no idea what you're talking about. Sit down and tell me what's going on."

Suddenly, Adriana wasn't sure she had made the right choice in coming here. She knew her place, and she knew if Tony hadn't called or come by, that was his prerogative. Jesus, what was she going to do next, call his wife, ring his damned doorbell? She doubted Mikey knew anything; he was on the outskirts of family business. Then again, he could be in on the whole thing, involved somehow or maybe even some sort of ringmaster trying to break her and Tony apart.

Suddenly, Adriana thought over her relationship with Tony. They had met two years ago, when she was Mikey's guest at a family Christening. She already knew a few of the guys there, since Mikey often took her out and showed her off, especially when he was hoping the relationship would become more serious. She didn't know any of the women, and she could almost feel them talking about her behind her back, glowering and glaring in true Jersey fashion. Suddenly, a strong hand gripped her shoulder and spun her around.

"Dance with me."

All it took were those three words. Adriana was stunned by the brazen demeanor of this handsome stranger, and also by the fact that he wasn't handsome in the conventional way. He was actually a bit on the short side, and certainly didn't boast a six-pack like Mikey did. "In fact," Adriana thought "the guy looks like he hasn't stepped foot in a gym in his entire life." This certainly wasn't the type of guy Adriana would have looked at twice, much less given the pleasure of her company on the dance floor, where she liked to think she was a pretty hot number. However, there was something overtly sexy about the man, he seemed to exude some type of power and Adriana was drawn in.

"HAHA! Don't you think I'm a little too young to be dancing with you? And don't you have a wife around here somewhere?"

Adriana tried to play cool, but she could feel her heart pounding. For God's sake, was she starting to sweat? She never, not in 24 years of her life, had this reaction to a man. He was only a man for God's sake! And why did she spew out that crap about a wife? Was she secretly hoping he didn't have one? Was she second-guessing herself? Jesus, what was going on?

"Don't worry about my wife; she's busy with her bitchy friends hidden in a corner gossiping about you. And don't worry about age because I can definitely keep up with you."

And he proved he could, in every area of life. He swept Adriana of her feet (literally) that day and in four years, nothing had changed. She was as crazy about Tony as she had been that day and she was not only pissed that she hadn't heard from him, she was worried. She loved him, and while she understood his family's code and that he would never leave his wife, a small part of her secretly wished he would. As ashamed as she was to admit it, that same small part often wished a deadly illness upon his wife, Delores. She dreamed of a wedding, a big fairytale affair, with all of her relatives and Tony's family standing by; the most powerful men in Jersey dancing at her wedding, this was her private dream. It was also one she knew would never be realized, and so she took whatever she could get, even if it meant stolen lunch hours and usually keeping her feelings a secret from Tony.

"You want me to tell you what's going on Mikey? I don't know what's going on. I haven't seen or heard from Tony in three days! You know that's not like him Mikey. Has he called you? Have you seen him? Have you heard anything?"

Adriana was aware that she sounded hysterical, but she really didn't give a damn right now. All she wanted were answers. Though now that she thought about it, perhaps Mikey wasn't the right person to ask. After all, hadn't he tried to steer her away from Tony from the get-go? Right at the Christening, in fact, when he tried to cut in on the dance, and countless other times over the last four years. In fact, it suddenly seemed to Adriana that the majority of her and Mikey's conversations over the past four years had been about Tony and why he wasn't the right guy for her. She always blew the conversations off as Mikey just running his mouth, but now she thought maybe they had more serious undertones; maybe whatever had befallen Tony had been Mikey's fault. Then again, maybe she was just watching too much Discovery I.D. before bed.

"I swear I haven't heard from him, and nobody's said anything at all, at least, not to me."

"Well, something's going on Mikey, this isn't like him at all and you know it."

"All right Ad, lemme get you some water or coffee. Sit back, take a breath, and when I get back, you tell me exactly what the hell is going on."

When Mikey left the room, Adriana tried to call Tony again, but to no avail. The phone went straight to voicemail, just as it had for the past three days. She took a breath, pulled out her lip gloss, and tried to pull herself together, despite her hysterical state of mind. After all, she had a reputation to uphold, she was a strong Jersey girl with important ties to some of the most powerful people in the state, and that had to count for something, didn't it? When Mikey got back, she would tell him what was going on, and he would help her figure out what to do.

Mikey returned with her coffee, light and sweet, just like he knew she liked it. He straightened out his Armani suit, closed his office door and took a seat behind his desk with his feet on it. He twirled a pen in his hand, a calm and casual demeanor about him.

"All right Ad, what's going on? This isn't like you at all."

Adriana took a deep breath and a sip of coffee. She tried to collect her thoughts so she was making sense, as opposed to prattling on like an idiot.

"Today's Wednesday Mikey. I haven't heard from Tony in three days. He called me Sunday night and I haven't heard from him since. Never mind him calling, but he hasn't come by my place and he hasn't stopped by Fiore's for lunch or dinner, and he knew I was working the past three days."

"And that's weird?"

"Yeah Mikey, it's friggin' weird. Tony calls me every day, usually four or five times, he always answers my calls or texts by the time Conan is on. He knows my schedule like he knows his own, and there's no way he's going to let three days go by without talking to or seeing me."

Adriana was aware that she was starting to sound hysterical again, but she really didn't care anymore. All she cared about was Tony and where he was. All right, that wasn't all she cared about, there was the tiny matter of the safe deposit box, but Tony was her main concern.

"Well, if you were my girlfriend, there is no way I'd go a day without seeing you, but of course, I'm not. I'm also not married with kids. Maybe he took some time off from his double life and decided to become a family man."

"Oh, up yours, Mikey! You know for a fact that Tony is the farthest thing from a faithfully married man. I'm not his first goomata, but I'm sure as shit gonna be his last. If you're not gonna help me figure this out, then I'm out and I'll do it myself. And don't think you or any of your buddies are gonna stop me."

Adriana feared she may have gone too far, as there was no point in alienating Mikey, especially since he was "in" in a way she never could be. She was just worried, about Tony and the damn box. Yes, she had to admit it, at least to herself, the box was a concern, but one she could deal with later. After all, there was no point in revealing *everything* to Mikey, all he had to do was help her find Tony.

"Jesus! Friggin relax. Of course I'll help you. I'm just trying to figure out what's going on. I swear I haven't heard anything and I sure as shit haven't seen anything. Don't go getting all pissy with me; you're the one who stormed in her like a friggin tornado spewing questions I just can't answer."

"I know Mikey, I know. I'm not sure what to do and I'm pretty sure you're the only one who can help me. You have to, you have to help me. You're the only one who will tell me the things I need to know and not treat me like a stupid goomata. I'm more than that to Tony, I know I am. I can't go asking any of the other guys, they'll just blow me off or tell me to take my ass home and wait like a good girl. That's not me Mikey, you know it isn't."

Adriana stared at Mikey, desperate for him to tell her something. She knew, especially after four years, that Tony didn't just decide to take his family on a vacation and leave her behind with only a hostessing job (and a part-time one at that) to support herself. He just wouldn't. Plus, Tony knew she wouldn't stand for that, she was a strong woman and she deserved his best, at least the best he could give considering his present situation. Jesus, he told her about the box, didn't he? That had to mean something.

She still wasn't sure that approaching Mikey had been the best decision. After all, he had tried to stop the relationship from progressing throughout the years. Besides the attempted cut-in at the Christening (thwarted quickly by several of Tony's friends), Mikey had tried unsuccessfully throughout the years to break the two up. His tactics ranged from drunken rants about how Adriana deserved so much more to making up stories about Tony with other women to flat-out telling Adriana to leave Tony and run away with him. The mafia code of keeping your hands off the girlfriend of another family member seemed to go right over Mikey's head. When it came to Adriana, he just didn't care. These thoughts led Adriana to believe that perhaps she had made a bad choice in coming to him with this.

"All right Ad, the guys are getting together at Fiore's tonight for a meeting. Meet me around the corner, we'll figure out how to get in there and maybe we'll hear something." "Thanks Mikey, you're a real friend. Call me when you get there and I'll come meet you outside."

Adriana jumped behind the wheel of her car, feeling somewhat better about her current situation. She felt like she really understood people, and she was sure if Mikey had anything to do with Tony being gone, she would have some inclination. She knew he wasn't thrilled with the situation, partly because he wanted Adriana for himself and also because he felt she deserved better. As his friend, she supposed she shouldn't complain about him wanting good things for her, but his desire for her was a little annoying, even after all these years.

What else annoyed Adriana at this point was the fact that the damn cat had a vet appointment. Naturally, she had a checking account set up by Tony, and paying the bill wouldn't be an issue, at least, not yet. Of course, she had to drive forty minutes out of her way to find a vet that would see an Elf cat, so rare that it hadn't been recognized by cat associations. Of course, when she told Tony she wanted a cat, he had to buy the best, the, an unrecognizable breed that could only be checked out by a vet who had three patients. Of course, even in his absence, Tony left his mark upon her.

"Fido, I'm home."

Adriana called out to the cat, the very cat that was infringing upon her afternoon. While she looked in all the regular hiding spots, the bathroom, under and behind the couch, and in the bedroom, she pondered the mysterious safe deposit box and tried to remember how she had become aware of its existence. She remembered Tony mentioning it one afternoon, how she would always be taken care of, and she would always have information that was worth money.

"Oh yeah, now you're playing sugar daddy for me? What do I have to do to earn this prize?"

"Nothing, Adriana. There is nothing you have to do. I want you to know that you mean so very much to me. Enough that I have made sure that you will have enough money to live your life the way you want, at least for a few years." Tony chuckled.

"How much money are you talking about, lover?"

"Enough, Adriana. There's enough cash. There are also stocks, bonds, CDs, and some very valuable information that not many people possess. If used correctly, that could certainly provide additional income for you, if need should arise."

"Jeez Tony, the only thing missing is a bar of gold!" Adriana tried to make a joke, a nervous habit. Tony knew it too.

"Stop, babe. Nothing is going to happen, and I'll always be around to take care of you. This is just an insurance policy for you."

But obviously, something had happened. She couldn't find Tony, couldn't talk to him, and most infuriatingly, she had no idea where the key to this mysterious box might be. That was another concern popping into her head: Did someone know that she knew about this box? Did someone think she had the key? Was she in danger? She didn't think Tony would do that intentionally, but all it would take in this world of danger and deceit would be the inkling of the thought that she knew more than she did. If Tony had mentioned that box to someone else, he could have put her in harm's way: the last thing he claimed he wanted to do. And, where was that damned cat?

After combing the house for Fido, she was more dumbfounded than ever. The cat wasn't under any beds, not in the shower, where he often liked to nap, and not on top of the fridge. She was stupefied however, when she walked back through the living room and saw Fido right on the couch, exactly where she had left him this morning. She growled audibly; was she now so involved within her own head that she completely ignored the cat sitting on the couch? Why hadn't he moved? The cat was usually prancing around the house, so jumpy and loud that Tony often asked her to lock the cat away when he came over.

"I guess we don't have to worry about that now, Fido, do we?" If she couldn't talk to Tony, she might as well talk to her cat.

They drove to the vet in silence, unheard of for Fido, who usually wailed the whole time he was in anyone's car. Adriana couldn't worry about Fido now, though something was clearly wrong. She had gotten a call from Mikey, who told her to meet him around the corner from Fiore's at 6 p.m. Adriana wondered how the family could possibly have a meeting during the dinner rush, but she quickly remembered the private room at the back of the restaurant. No wonder she was always told to keep customers waiting rather than seat them there.

"Pieces are coming together, Fido" she said with certainty, though there was no reply.

The vet's office was quiet, but this was to be expected since there were only three patients on his client list. Of course, Tony had found the vet for her, so who knew what the hell was really going on? After the preliminary check-in, the two went through the usual rigmarole of niceties. Adriana revealed to Dr. DeRose that Fido had been behaving strangely, not eating as much, and was generally lethargic (more so than usual for an Elf cat, or any cat for that matter). The doctor seemed to feel that Fido was going through a phase, that all would return to normal (after all, cats, especially rare breeds were of a certain nature) and that if things didn't return to normal in a few days, she should call and return with Fido for a more detailed check-up.

"Jesus Fido, couldn't you have anything really wrong with you? At least that would justify the trip."

Adriana was annoyed by the trip, the vet, and most of all, with Tony for this whole situation. She was rushing to get home, especially since it was already four thirty, and she would need to find something appropriate for a stakeout. She didn't know exactly what that would entail, but she imagined something black and sporty (in case she needed to take off running). She certainly never envisioned this situation when she twirled across the dance floor with the man who was at once the love of her life and the thorn in her side.

Adriana parked in the underground garage, took Fido in her arms, entered her apartment and deposited the cat on the couch. She headed to the bedroom to get dressed; passing pictures of her and Tony on the beach in Aruba, skiing in Aspen, and hamming it up with Mickey Mouse in Disney World. Memories, her memories, created with a man who disappeared like a thief in the night. She was determined to find out what happened to him, come hell or high water. She knew she was putting herself and possibly Mikey, in a dangerous situation. Other goomatas would probably let this go, but she couldn't. She loved Tony, and what's more, she had no idea how to get to the box.

Dressed in black, Adriana headed to Fiore's on foot. She felt prepared, as so many of the crime busters she had read about undertook surveillance this way. The restaurant was a neighborhood staple; family (in both senses of the word) owned and operated for over forty years. Adriana had gotten the job through Tony's affiliation with Joey Fiore, another member of the family. Joey was a great boss; he knew how important Tony was in the family, and therefore, how important it was to keep Adriana happy. Her schedule was made by her, every week. She gave herself as few or as many hours as she wanted, took vacations when she felt like it, and made three times more than the other hostesses, one was a ninety-year-old neighbor who had seen the building constructed and the other was Joey's thirteen-year-old niece, who was working her way up to waitress. While she knew Joey liked her, Adriana also knew that she would be in more trouble than simply being out of work if she was caught spying with Mikey.

Even this knowledge didn't stop her, and Adriana walked with renewed purpose to Fiore's. She met Mikey outside on the corner, and they two discussed their plan of action.

"Listen Ad, you know this place better than I do. What's the best way for us to get close to the room at the back without being seen?"

Adriana thought for a moment and replied, "Through the side kitchen door. There's a storage closet on the left side of the back room door. We just have to get in that closet without being seen.

Armed with this knowledge, the unlikely pair set off to gain information. Adriana wasn't sure she would hear anything useful and wasn't sure how much she trusted Mikey, but she had little choice at this point; she had to track down her boyfriend. Getting into the kitchen through the side door was a no-brainer, as Wednesday nights were staffed by only one chef, who was half blind and deaf to boot. As the family members removed their coats and handed them to Joey to be put in the front closet, Adriana and Mikey saw their opportunity and ran with it. They silently slunk around the doorway after Joey finished, and made their way into the closet, close enough that Adriana could smell the shoe polish on Mikey's uber-expensive shoes.

The conversation of the family sounded like the same Adriana had heard at a million dinners and parties. The men spoke briefly about what they should order, arguing between an appetizer of calamari or scungilli. The decision was made (scungilli) and the conversation moved on. The men discussed their business ventures, who owed them money and what they would do about it, and what they might undertake next. Adriana was on the verge of napping when she heard someone utter Tony's name and felt Mikey jab her in the side, motioning towards the door as though she were as deaf as the chef, and while she couldn't tell who was saying what, she was certain they were discussing Tony.

"Where the hell is that sonofabitch?"

"He called me Sunday during dinner, I told him to call me back, but he never did."

"His wife won't stop calling me."

"Somebody needs to get on that."

"Where's the box?"

The mention of the box certainly got Adriana's attention. It was just as she feared, someone else knew about the box, someone with a lot more power than she had.

"What box? What's in the effin' box?"

"No idea, sir. I just know that somewhere there's a box and something is in it."

"What's in it? What the hell are you talking about? Why didn't anybody feel this was important to mention when this bastard went missing?"

That voice Adriana knew. That was certainly Charlie Beans, the head of the family. If he used the word "missing" Adriana believed that the family didn't have anything to do with Tony's disappearance. It wasn't a guarantee, but she was going to trust her gut once again. Adriana felt a bit better. Clearly, nobody knew the details of the box the way she did. However, the sheer fact that someone else knew about it made her very, very nervous.

The meal ended, and the family members headed to the front of the restaurant to get their coats and hats. Adriana and Mikey waited until the room was silent and crept from the closet and out of the kitchen door. They looked at each other and giggled out of sheer relief when they got outside and under the light of the moon. They weren't yet sure what happened to Tony, but they were both pretty sure the family didn't have anything to do with it. Adriana was also sure that they knew about the box, but less of its contents than she did. Unfortunately, it seemed as though nobody knew where to find this box. As she began to head home, with Mikey walking her like a gentleman, Adriana heard a voice call out to her.

"Goodnight Adriana. Good night Mikey. You two kids have a good night."

Adriana began to shake with fear. That voice belonged to Charlie Beans and the two of them were directly behind the restaurant dressed in black, looking like two idiots playing detective. While Mikey was a detective, Adriana couldn't claim the same, and her worries began to increase.

"What's wrong, Ad? You're not worried about Charlie are you? So what? We were out for a walk together. There's nothing strange about that."

"Are you kidding, Mikey? We happen to be right by the restaurant at exactly the same time all these guys are leaving? We're dressed like two extras from the *Men in Black* movies and there's nothing strange about that? We're screwed."

There was nothing to be said or done. The situation was what it was, and the only way to figure out exactly how much the family knew would be to wait it out. Mikey offered to stay on the couch, and Adriana gladly took him up on the offer. She knew many women who would refuse, but she wasn't one of them. The two walked in to find Fido still sitting on the couch.

"Hey Ad, what's up with Fido?"

"No idea Mikey, I should probably call the vet again tomorrow. The damn cat hasn't made a peep since Monday morning. You hungry? How about some eggplant?"

The night passed fitfully for Adriana: still no word from Tony, but at least she and Mikey were still alive. The two had coffee, and Mikey headed back to his office, promising to catch up with Adriana later or if he received any new information. Adriana cleaned up some tissues that Fido had nibbled on, along with papers and socks. Apparently, the only thing Fido didn't want to eat was cat food. She put in another call to Dr. DeRose and headed out to his office with a once-again silent Fido.

After the required niceties (weren't these passé by now?), Dr. DeRose decided to take some x-rays, especially since Fido hadn't been meowing, crying, or eating. The non-use of the litter box was also a concern, so Adriana signed consent forms and immediately thought of calling Tony. When she remembered that he wouldn't answer, she opted to call Mikey instead. As much as she complained about Fido and his eccentricities, she really did love the cat and all it had come to represent. Mikey agreed to drive the forty minutes to offer his support, though he really wasn't an animal person and didn't get it.

Mikey and Adriana sat in the waiting room while Dr. DeRose read the x-rays. He emerged a short time later, with the pictures in one hand and a small envelope in the other.

"Well Adriana, we're all finished here, at least for today."

"Where's Fido? Is he ok? How were the x-rays?" Adriana once again found herself just shy of hysterical.

"Fido's in the back resting. The x-ray showed a small blockage in the esophagus, which wasn't significant enough to constrict breathing, but made eating nearly impossible."

Adriana closed her eyes and took a deep breath. "Are you telling me my cat swallowed something? That's the big problem? My cat swallowed something that led to surgery?"

"Yes," Dr. DeRose replied. He dropped the x-rays on the table and emptied the contents of the envelope into his hand.

"Does this look familiar?" He asked the duo, holding up a small key.

"You have to be effing kidding me...my cat swallowed the key?" Adriana screamed, at once relieved that half the mystery had been solved but also irritated that Tony still hadn't been found.

"Yup, it seems your cat may have a taste for Bank of America safe deposit boxes" Dr. DeRose replied.

"How do you know it's Bank of America?" Adriana asked in amazement.

"It's imprinted on a tiny tag attached to the top." Dr. DeRose looked as confused as Adriana was feeling.

"Thanks Doc. We have to be going." Adriana began pulling Mikey out of the office, a death grip on the key she had grabbed from the vet's hand.

"Wait, wait! Fido needs to be picked up tomorrow."

"Sure Doc, sure thing!"

Adriana and Mikey made their way to Bank of America. At the front desk, Adriana was asked to show her identification, and upon approval, was taken to a back room. She had pictured walls and walls of boxes, but was told by the branch manager that that was not the case for "special clients." After placing the box in front of Adriana, the manager left her alone to open the box, facing a very uncertain future by herself.

As she opened the box and saw all the cash, all the paperwork and the vast fortune in front of her, Adriana realized none of it meant anything without Tony. He was all she wanted, and as she thought over the past four years, tears began to run down her face. She was ready to place the top on the box when a slip of bright pink paper caught her eye. She had just placed the new notepad next to the phone on Saturday, when Tony came by after work. She quickly picked up the paper and read:

Hey Baby. I am heading out of town for a few days. I need to regroup and talk to a lawyer down in the Keys. I think it's about time to worry about my own happiness and what I want. I'm going to ask Delores for a divorce so we can move forward with our life together. I didn't want to wake you, so I decided to leave the safe-deposit key on the dining room table, but I guess you figured that out. I'll be back Thursday morning, and I can't wait to see you! Love, Tony

Adriana shook her head in disbelief, it was like a dream come true. Everything was going to be fine, though she might kill Fido with her bare hands. She took notice of a small arrow on the bottom of the paper, an indicator to turn it over. She did and read:

P.S. The effin' cat is jumping all over the place. You have to think about doing something with this sonofabitch!

Adriana laughed out loud, grabbed the note, and headed out to tell Mikey what had happened, the smile from a dream fulfilled never leaving her face.

2012

Hannon, Inc.

The Case of the Cat Lady and the Junkyard Dog

Daniel S. Helwig

It's a thin piece of brushed aluminum that runs across the front of the windshield, along the bottom. It looks like chrome, but it's not; about an inch wide, sits between the windshield and the body of the car. Mine's missing," I said.

Butch Renninger looked at me, but you could tell he was seeing something else in his mind. It was his junkyard. I'd been here before, trying to collect various pieces for a '68 Dodge Dart convertible. Butch was about 5' 7" – a guess since I'd never seen him off his stool and out from behind the counter. He was roundish, always wearing a white t-shirt that had grease and dirt and whatever stains all over it, with thick, pink arms sticking out, ending in hands that looked like they'd never been clean, never would be. And dark green Dickies work pants. A cigarette hung from his mouth, dangling at a 45 degree angle. His face always seemed to have several days of facial hair growth, same color as his orange mop of hair on top, covered by a baseball cap – "USMC – Once a Marine, Always a Marine, Semper Fi."

His shop was an old travel trailer. It was hot as hell in there and smelled like gasoline, rubber and stale cigarettes. On what used to be the bench for the dinner table was a stack of wheels from a '70 Monte Carlo; on a top bunk bed was a row of radios removed from early '80s GM vehicles – in-dash 8 track models. Over in the corner was an engine – looked like a small-block Chevy but I couldn't say for sure. You could never tell if the stuff had been there a year or 10 minutes, but you had a feeling Butch could inventory the whole place with his eyes shut.

"You been here before. You know where they are," he said. "Top of the hill, east end. There's a couple late '60s Dodges out there. Not sure about that piece." His phone rang and he made it clear we were done.

You didn't run an auto salvage yard on a winsome personality. I liked him anyway.

It was about a 15-minute walk to the top of the hill, through orchard grass and rows and rows of junk cars, some late models and some 50-plus years old. It was a Friday morning and a glorious one at that. Early May in Pennsylvania was a feast for the senses. Today would end up in the mid 80s, but for now it was cool, sunny, the grass was wet from morning dew. It looked like I had the place to myself.

A junkyard. Old cars with spider webs of cracked windshields where you could see the occupants' heads had hit the glass in an era before seatbelts. Dead cars. Hoods up, an expired look. Wheels off, some with trees and bushes growing around and even up through the engine compartments. I found the Dodges; there were a couple of convertibles. Their tops were in rags and they reminded me of old-fashioned baby carriages. No '68s, but there was a '67, and the part I was searching for should have been the same on the'67. I walked over to it. Something in the grass caught my eye; a snake slithered away and I remembered my dad's admonition about May and sunny days and rattle snakes. More carefully now, I cleared the area around the Dodge. The part I needed had already been scavenged by somebody else.

I set the toolbox I was carrying in the grass and used it as a seat, looking down the hill and across the valley. Butch's 50 acres of automotive relics formed the morning side of the valley.

A road ran along the bottom of the vee, and opposite the junkyard was a horse farm. From here, they looked like a mix of Thoroughbreds with a few Arabians mixed in. From my perch, I could see a guy walk out onto his porch. It was a beautiful spread, and I imagined the guy came out every morning whistling the theme from "The Magnificent Seven." It looked for all the world like he was staring straight at me, half-a-mile away.

A loud boom sounded like the report of a deer rifle; the horses spooked and ran around in their pasture. Apparently the machine that crushes cars in the junkyard had caught one with something still flammable in the tank. Going out with a bang. The guy across the valley shook his head and walked back in his house.

I took a last look at the '67. A front-end collision. It was white, black top, black interior. I noticed that the radio knobs were in better shape than mine. How does chrome-plated plastic sit exposed to the elements and survive? Anyway, I took them off and walked down the hill to Butch's hut.

"No luck, but I got these off a '67. How much?" I said.

"Eight bucks," he said. It seemed like a lot for 30-year-old plastic, but I wasn't going to find the knobs at K-mart. I gave him a ten and he pulled out a wad of bills two inches thick and gave me two singles.

Commerce, junkyard style

I threw the knobs in the glove box, took off my coveralls and put them in the trunk, and started the Dodge. I was alternatively driving and restoring the Dart, depending on the day and the money supply. I'm a private detective, and in the private detective game, when you have no clients, you have time to work on old cars, but if you have time to work on old cars, you have no money. The Dart was therefore a work in progress and probably always would be. The paint was a faded green, the chrome pitted, the car itself sound and solid.

I drove the 20 minutes into town and parked on the street in front of my office, "Hannon, Inc.," in part to give some evidence that there was a business located there. I had a place that fronted Main Street in Shade Mountain, a town of 10,000 people that backed up against the Appalachian Mountains. Like many Pennsylvania towns, this one started life as a farming village in the 18th century, acquired a small college in the late 19th century courtesy of a religious denomination with some bold dreams, became a lumbering hub in the early 20th century, and was spending the latter couple years of the 20th century fighting for survival. Farming had consolidated, lumber came from elsewhere, any regional manufacturing was gone or about to go, and it looked like we were all going to earn our living selling Amway to each other. President Clinton told us in the last election that NAFTA would be helping us all out any day now but so far, nada. Not in Shade Mountain.

And not much call for a private detective in a small town, but I'd wandered into the work after college. I'd gone to school here at Apollonia University and gotten a degree in comparative religion, but worked in the Campus Safety office to pay the tuition. Turned out that I liked putting the pieces together of the various infractions and indiscretions that occur between and among 18-22 year olds. After school, I didn't really want to teach or preach, or go on to grad school, or even be a cop, and I'd probably just seen too many "Spenser for Hire" TV shows for my own good. At one time, I thought I might work with my dad; he was a land surveyor and taught me the finer points of geometry before he died during my senior year of high school from cancer he thought he probably developed spraying fruit orchards with DDT as a kid. Mom moved to Florida a few years ago after my siblings decided their futures and their fortunes were not going to be made watching the rust belt oxidize. They say a liberal arts degree teaches you how to think. So sure, I can think now. I think I may be just about broke.

Mornings, I had a woman, Dottie Fisher, come in to answer the phones and keep track of filing, and generally give the impression that this was a going concern, plus give me someone to spar with verbally. Dottie was probably 60, born and raised in Shade Mountain, wiry with angular features, brown hair that had stayed the color and style of 1963 Jackie Kennedy. She had a perpetual look of disgust on her face. As a teenager, I helped out at a horse farm and the word that came to mind with Dottie was "mare-ish," defined as bossy in a uniquely feminine way. I walked into the office, knowing Dottie would be ready to let me have it for something. "Thanks for stopping by, Bryce," she said as I opened the door. "So nice that you occasionally make it here by noon."

"Gosh, Dottie, I hope you weren't worried," I said. "I'll bet you were here wringing your hands. Any calls?"

"No calls. And you don't pay me enough to just assume that I'll cover for you when someone shows up wanting to speak with you and you're nowhere to be found."

"Are you saying we have a client in the house, Ms. Fisher?" I said with feigned, but some, actual disbelief.

"She's in your office, Sherlock. I shoulda told her that I didn't know if or when you'd be in, but I told her you were out on a case and I expected you. She said she'd wait. Yes, she's pretty. In case that's what you're wondering." She smirked, a look that came naturally to her.

"What I'm wondering is if you made coffee," I said.

"I did," she said. "And I drank it," she said. And she smirked.

She had hair the color of beach sunshine. I couldn't help but notice the way it fell around her pretty face. And onto the floor. She was standing on her head. I may not know much, but I know that when a beautiful blonde is standing on her head in my office, it's going to be an interesting day. I mean, I think of myself as a feminist. I voted for Mondale/Ferraro. I've been trained not to think of women as sex objects. But these were nice legs. No, check that; these were perfect legs, the kind of legs that heretofore had only existed speculatively. And I had a good, long look at them, seeing how I was basically face-to-face with her sterling silver anklet.

"Perspective is important in my line of work," I said. "But I'll admit I never thought of looking at life from that viewpoint." How charming of me.

She righted herself as quickly as a gymnast. She wore a worried look and her eyes were red. I wasn't sure if it was from the blood rushing to her head or whether she'd been crying.

"Mr. Hannon. My name is Melissa Sherwood," she said as we shook hands. "I started work this semester at the University and haven't met too many people. My field of study is interpretive dance and I was just using a yoga pose to clear my head, waiting for you to arrive. Do you do yoga?"

Hmm. Of course I'd never done yoga. The closest I'd been to yoga was... well, I could spell it. Yet, I said, "I've always been fascinated with yoga. I've read everything I can get my hands on about it, but there hasn't been much yoga expertise in Shade Mountain, and it seems like yoga isn't something you can easily teach yourself." I glanced at the door to make sure it was closed; if Dottie heard me, she would probably make a noise like vomiting. She was that kind of helpful.

"You need a strong core to do many of the poses. It's very hard work, excellent exercise," she said.

I could see that Melissa Sherwood had a strong core. And now I noticed that pretty face connected to a neck that was indescribably fine, the collar bone delicately peeking out of her white "A U is 4 U" t-shirt.

"Well Ms. Sherwood, or is it Dr. Sherwood? Apart from edification that I no doubt would find very worthwhile, how can I help you?" I said as I leaned against my desk to steady myself.

She lost her sangfroid and sank into a chair in front of me. "It's just Melissa, and this is going to sound silly, but it's my dog," she said. "He's a boxer, Jack, and I've had him for 10 years. He's everything to me, and he's been missing for two days."

A lost dog. It had come to that. Four years of college to find lost pets. Granted, a lost pet of a gorgeous woman, perfectly fit, an educator, with a strong core, but still. I could hear my dad in my head asking why I hadn't majored in math, become an actuary or something.

"Ms. Sherwood – Melissa - I'm terribly sorry for you," I said as I sat down, thinking, "OK, Whatever. I'll let her down easy and wish her the best in her search for poor Fido." Then I looked in her eyes and there was something so vulnerable and beautiful and powerful all at the same time. Speech became a challenge. "That's bad," I offered, proof that one syllable words are a good fallback in these situations.

"I'm sure this is outside your normal scope," she said, "but the reality is I don't know that many people here, the police would never help with something like a lost pet, and I just don't know where to turn. You have no idea how much Jack means to me." Those eyes were killing me. And her voice had this liquid quality, like ... some sort of liquid. The wet kind.

"Wow," I said, now finding the whole subject–verb combination a challenge.

And then she said, "Of course I assume you'll need a retainer. Would $1,000 be enough to start?"

"Uh... $1,000," I replied in a measured way. I was suddenly beginning to see daylight, cognitively speaking. A new top for the Dart was $600, installed.

She showed me a picture she'd brought along. The thing with boxers is that they look very much like other boxers. Like a "67 Dart looks like a '68. If you know how to spot the difference, you can see it right away. Jack had the classic good looks of the breed, but no distinguishing characteristics. Still, how many boxers did I see in Shade Mountain in the last month? I thought the job was within my scope.

"Melissa, I'll admit that this isn't the type of work I usually undertake, but as they say, you may be the exception that proves the rule." I smiled, indicating that this was me being clever.

I gave Dottie a $1,000 check and told her we had a case.

"Mmmm. Hmmm..." she said. "Anything I should be aware of? Can I start on any research?

"It's a challenging case and I'll need some time to think," I said.

"You want me to deposit this, while you 'think,' Sherlock?" she said.

"You say that with healthy skepticism," I said. "Something you care to share?"

"So sensitive," she said. "You want to open up a lost pet agency, why do I care? You pay me to answer the phones, not to be skeptical."

"Couldn't have said it better myself, Dottie. In fact, I was also trying to remember why I pay you, so thanks for that helpful reminder," I said.

"Of course," she said, "I'll be sure to let my neighbors know you're the guy to call if they end up with a cat up a tree, or a hamster that won't run on its wheel, or a dead parrot. She smiled that smile of hers that made me wonder what side of the employee-employer relationship she thought she was on.

I remembered that the '67 Dart in Butch's junkyard was an automatic, like mine, but that his '67 had a center console which dressed up the interior nicely. It wasn't perfect, but it was pretty nice, and now that I had cash, I wanted it. I decided to go out to his junkyard that afternoon to see how much it would take for him to part with it.

"Back again," Butch said. "You make me an offer on that '67 so you can take all the parts you want off it."

"You don't want to get rid of your stock," I said. I noticed a dog dish hubcap upside down over in the corner, then saw that it was being used as an actual dog dish, then noticed the dog.

"Hell," he said. "Between the DEP and that goddamn neighbor, I'd be better off selling it all. Come on J.R.," he called to the dog.

"Department of Environmental Protection not a fan of classic cars?" I said. J.R. was a nice dog, well-cared for. "When'd you get the dog?"

"Watching him for a friend. The wife has cats and I'm catching hell for it. I said, fine, he'll stay with me all day. DEP sends more goddamn regulations every week. Drain the gas tanks, drain the oil, tires in a separate area, you name it. It's like I'm a goddamn baby killer or something," he said. "But it's that goddamn neighbor with the ponies has his britches twisted. Moves in last year and thinks he ought to be able to put me out of business. I was here before him. Let him bitch."

"He's got a nice place," I said. "Maybe he'd buy you out for a big number."

"He can go to hell," Butch said. "Whatchu need."

We agreed on a price - $75 – before I went up to take a look at the console and I peeled off the cash to add to his wad. He took a phone call from what sounded like his wife. Just a guess; I'm not married, but it sounded like a running argument with a generous helping of heat. I waved so-long and went up to remove the piece from the '67. It turned out to be tougher than it looked since the screws holding it to the transmission housing had 30 years of rust keeping them in place. Plus you had to take the front seats out to get to the thing.

I was on taking out the passenger seat when I heard another sound like a shot or a boom. Instinctively, I looked across at the horse farm. The horses took off nervously. Plus, I saw what looked like three or four dogs that looked like boxers spilling off of the porch, chasing each other around and acting like boxers do, which is to say… crazy. I didn't think much of it, but I did think of Melissa Sherwood. From this distance, I couldn't see them well enough to compare them mentally to the picture Melissa had given me. But hey, lots of people like boxers, and, I mean, everybody who has boxers can't suddenly become a suspect, right? And who's to say that someone even took her boxer. But seriously, was I going to start seeing boxers everywhere now?

I finally got the console off and still had some skin on my knuckles. I carried it down to show Butch. I opened the door to the trailer and he was slumped over the counter, dead. I may not know much, but I know that when a troll-like junkyard owner is slumped over dead with a bullet hole in his head and my $75 still in his right hand, it's going to be an interesting day. I lifted Butch's heavy head. His eyes were still open. He was definitely dead. And come to think of it, no J.R.

I looked around the place. What used to be windows in the trailer were now just openings, so someone could have shot into the trailer from a distance pretty easily. There was a ledger under the counter and I saw that Butch had just written "console '67 Dodge - $75." I'll be damned. The guy kept records.

I walked out of the trailer to get myself together. No other cars were around but mine. For the first time noticed a neat, small ranch house about two hundred yards away from the junkyard. I must have overlooked it before, too captivated by old Chryslers. It was like an oasis of pretty in a sea of ugly. I decided I needed to see if there was a Mrs. Butch.

There literally was a white picket fence around the yard of the place. The grass was well-kept, tulips were up around the sidewalk and there was a good-sized flowering cherry tree in bloom. A blue gazing ball in the yard like my grandmother had when I was growing up. It was a rancher with white brick half-way up the side of the house, gray siding and black shutters around a big bay window, through which a black and white tuxedo cat was eyeing me. I was on a concrete slab porch, with metal furniture painted pink, and copper wind chimes were making some music off to the side. I rang the bell.

Mrs. Renninger couldn't have been more unlike Butch. She was putting in a left earring – gold and exquisite looking – as she answered the door. She was probably 55, 5' 4", trim figure, short brown hair coiffed neatly, a black pants suit on. Blue eyes that matched a sapphire necklace around her neck. It looked like she was on her way to the club to play bridge. A second cat – a white Siamese – brushed against my Levis.

"Hello. Mrs. Renninger?" I started. It's hard to know how to tell someone that a loved one is dead, and being only a slight acquaintance of the recently deceased doesn't make it easier, I was finding. Plus, I looked like… well, like I was working in a junkyard. "I was here to buy a part for my car, and when I went back to see your husband, I found that he'd been shot. It appears that he's dead," I said. "I'm sorry to be the one to tell you this and I assume you'll want to contact the police immediately and I offer my condolences and obviously I'll help in any and every way that I can." I stopped, partially to catch my breath and partially because she had turned her back to me and was walking to the kitchen and seemed not to be listening to me.

"Would you like some coffee?" she said.

"I beg your pardon??" I said, unsure which of us was having a delusion.

"I said would you care for some coffee?"

"Uh. Yes?" I said. "Mrs. Renninger, perhaps you didn't hear me, but …"

"Cream and sugar?" she asked.

"Please. But…"

"I heard you. You said someone shot the filthy bastard," she said. "You said he's dead. So I assume there is no rush. He'll still be dead after we drink this coffee."

She handed me a mug of coffee that was the color of a brown wingtip shoe – perfect. This was weird in the extreme, but something told me to play through this stretch. She collected a handful of other jewelry that was on the counter and carried it back the hallway, I assumed to a bedroom. I took a sip and looked around the place. I was sitting at an island that separated the kitchen and the living room. The place looked like a Mr. Clean commercial. Spotless. Oak floors in the hallways, tasteful decorations, a white kitchen with black and white checkerboard flooring. The living room had light green walls the color of sea grass and had a sofa that looked like the dog's sweater in *No Roses for Harry*, a children's book that was one of my favorites as a kid. The two cats were trying to get my attention. But there were at least half a dozen white ceramic cats with blue eyes all around the place. Here's one on the counter. There's one on a book shelf. A door-stop. Perched on a side-table. Identical. Life sized.

"You must like cats," I said.

"They apparently like you," she said, as the two cats jumped to the island and were attempting to get me to pet them. I'm not a cat person, but was attempting civilities, keeping things cordial if you will.

"Yes, but I was noticing the ceramics…"

"Oh," she said. "Yes, I started doing ceramics a few years ago and got stuck on cats. I hand paint them and then take them to get fired. I haven't been able to stop. They aren't exactly art, but they have great value to me." She handed me one. It was heavier than it looked and had a rattle to it.

"Mrs. Renninger, I believe we should call the police, and quickly," I said.

She blew over her coffee cup to cool the black liquid. "I suppose you're right," she said. "It is an inconvenience, though. Did you kill Butch?"

I spilled some of my coffee onto the counter. "No. I just found him, Mrs. Renninger." "It's Mary Jane," she said. "And of course you didn't kill him. Although many people wanted to see Butch dead, and I'd be close to the top of the list.

I was sitting at the bar at McCleary's Tavern that night, finishing off their Shepherd's Pie and drinking a beer. I was telling Mike McCarty about my day. Mike's probably my oldest friend. He was an adjunct professor who taught chemistry at AU when I was in school. He'd come to Shade Mountain in retirement because he thought the town was quaint and the housing was cheap compared to Morristown, New Jersey, where he taught at the Morristown Beard School, a swanky private K-12 school. Mike was about as Irish Catholic as they come. His folks had come to New York when he was four years old. He had dual citizenship.

I told Mike how I had left Mary Jane Renninger and walked down to the car as she was dialing the police. They arrived about 30 minutes later, sirens blaring, as if they could do something about the whole thing if they made enough noise. Mary Jane never came out of the house. Some customers had arrived and I had told them that there had been an emergency, the yard was closed. Amy Gregson was in charge of the case for the police. We had been in high school together and dated for about a year on and off. It was odd, now, working with her. I was finding it hard to have a professional relationship with someone I used to call "Cutie Baby."

Bryce my boy," he said. "You gotta quit driving around these old heaps. The problem is you need a new car." Leave it to Mike to draw a false correlation and make it my fault. There was a ball game on. Mike was a Yankees fan and they were playing the Orioles. A tie game, fifth inning. The bar was a dark, friendly place. Clean, good food, not fancy, but not a place that somebody from out of town would find. Not in the AAA book.

"Bet you $10 the Yankees win," Mike said.

"You still owe me $10 from last fall when we bet that they'd beat Cleveland in the Wildcard," I said.

"I'd rather owe you than cheat you," he said.

"Fine," I said. "You can work it off. I need some help on Monday for a few hours in the morning."

"Chuck you Farley," he said. "I'm retired. That means I don't work. Period."

"OK, just come with me for a hike then," I said. "Think of it as leisure activity."

I woke up at 6:30 AM out of habit Saturday morning. I rent a half house about three miles outside of town. When Shade Mountain had been lumber territory around the 1920s, the company had put up two dozen stick-built two-story homes along PA Route 56. They were not much, not insulated, cold in the winter, hot in the summer, but cheap to rent. I read the morning paper and drank coffee. The *Shade Mountain Messenger* said Butch had $5,000 in cash on him at the time he was shot. It also said that under the counter they found five kilos of cocaine. I believed the part about the cash, but I couldn't believe the dope. Six hundred wrecks in his backyard with six hundred trunks, six hundred glove boxes, six hundred nooks and crannies to hide bad stuff. It didn't add up that he'd keep it under a counter.

Maybe it was just a gut feeling, maybe it was too many kindred conversations about how hard it is to find small bolt pattern fourteen inch steel wheels for a Dodge, maybe it was the way he reminded me of why I stayed in Shade Mountain; the place had good people who worked hard and kept their noses clean but got their fingernails dirty. It was a hunch, but I had a feeling somebody put the cocaine in there while I was at the Renninger house. Police believed this was a drug murder, and who didn't want to see a drug distributor shot? Amy didn't mention the drugs when we spoke at the scene, either because she was being a trained professional or because she was trying not to remember the time we drank a whole bottle of Boone's Farm out of Dixie cups.

I took apart the Dart's ignition system. It had developed a miss and I'd already replaced the points. Twice. I battled with the timing light, re-gapped the points, and cleaned the distributor again. Still no luck. Then I remembered that I had money. I went to the auto parts store and bought a new electronic ignition module; why mess with the points? The module was a 3"x4" steel box that mounted to the firewall and took 20 minutes to install. It was "new old stock," meaning that it was the actual part that Chrysler Motor Company put on 1970 and later Darts, so it was still relatively authentic. The Dart sounded perfect when I was done and I had that sense of accomplishment that's so evasive in modern life.

I was cleaning up when Amy Gregson stopped in. I asked her if she wanted some coffee and we went inside and I brewed another pot. We were both now in our mid-30s. She looked as good as a woman can look in a police uniform. She'd kept in shape. She had short gun-barrel-black hair, green eyes, and she was taller than most. Back in high school, she played basketball, and our senior year the team won the district championship. She also was good at the biathlon. Very good. I thought she could have gone to the Olympics, but she argued that she didn't have the money it took to take all that time off and train for something that might or might not work out. Amy always worried about money back then. And she usually had a serious look on her face. Now, she was wearing that same look.

"You were the last person to see Butch," she said. "What happened?"

"Amy, I told you what I know," I said. "but the cocaine was not there when I saw Butch after he was shot." I was playing my hunch. I had told her about finding Butch and told her about telling Mrs. Renninger. For some reason, I didn't tell her about Mrs. Renninger's invitation for coffee or her curious behavior.

"That doesn't make sense, Bryce," she said. "And Mrs. Renninger says she was worried that he was involved with drugs."

"Mrs. Renninger said that?" I said. "You talked to her?"

"Yes," Amy said. "She was in pretty rough shape when I saw her, but she said she tried to get Butch to tell her what was going on."

"She was in rough shape," I said. I was beginning to think I'd slipped into an episode of "Twin Peaks." Amy went on to say that the bullet that killed Bruce was from a Winchester 30-30, a standard deer rifle. There were probably hundreds of 30-30s in town. Deer hunting is a big pastime here in P-A, so the department was pretty much at a dead end with ballistics info.

So basically Amy thought I just missed seeing the cocaine, and she thought Mrs. Renninger was a grieving widow. I remembered that we broke up because we didn't see the world the same way.

That afternoon I went to see Melissa Sherwood. She rented an apartment on University Avenue, just a few blocks from AU. I wanted to get more of her story, see if she had any other pictures of her dog, and get over the fact that I couldn't form sentences in her company. She had a second floor three-room place, and the easiest way to get there was up a back staircase that was more or less a fire escape. It ended on a little outdoor porch and we sat there drinking more coffee. I was on about six cups at this point, and my leg had developed a twitch. I thought I could actually feel my brain vibrating.

Melissa said that she had come to AU in 1996 after getting a Master in Fine Arts in dance from the University of Colorado, Boulder. Her family was in Colorado, but she'd been so pleased to get the job, and they were happy for her. She had three younger brothers and her mom and dad had both worked for IBM, which had a big operation in Boulder. The family had boxers since she was a kid, and it had really become a Sherwood family crisis that her dog was missing. I began to see that this wasn't just a lost dog; this was a link to home.

She had last seen Jack at the office on Wednesday. Her chair had said she could bring Jack to work, so long as he stayed quiet, stayed in her office, and didn't cause a disturbance. She said the chair also had boxers and she felt that was a plus when she interviewed, felt they'd have something in common. Wednesday at 11:00 AM, she left for class, left Jack in the office but never thought to lock the door, and she came back and he was gone.

I asked her about the adjustment to AU. She said that the other faculty were dismissive. The Creative Arts Department had consolidated three years ago, likely because of budget cuts, and now included music, performance, theatre, and fine arts. The academy is like the Westminster Dog Show sometimes. It's a place that makes more out of what's on your diploma than what's in your head. An MFA is not considered as high a pedigree as a Ph.D. So there was a lot of snottiness and snarky behavior towards her, even more than usual. Twelve faculty members, plus she made thirteen. It was a tenure-track slot, but she got the sense that some of her peers would be hoping to find any way to derail that. I remembered that my advisor in school once said of higher education that the politics were so vicious because the stakes were so low.

I asked about the chair. She said his name was Randy Voxstall. He was apparently hired as chair as part of the consolidation; she said most people found him aloof. She had told him about Jack being missing when she got back to her office and he intimated that it must be her fault, that she was careless. Sounded like Mr. Personality.

She said that there was an end-of-year "forced fun" picnic tomorrow at his horse farm that she was definitely not looking forward to. Something told me I should offer to take her; it might have been my libido and it might have been my professional duty. At this point, I wondered if they were converging. I wasn't sure I could stop that from happening, and I wasn't sure it would be such a bad thing if it did. She was that kind of pretty.

That evening I drove out past the junkyard, partly to see if the ignition module worked at highway speeds and partly to get another look at scene. I stopped along the side of the road outside Butch's junkyard; it was a straight view into Butch's trailer. Anybody who was a decent shot with a deer rifle with a scope could have taken Butch out.

Sunday was a beautiful day for a picnic. A light breeze, temperature about 75 degrees, and not a cloud in the sky. I washed the Dart and vacuumed the interior. The picnic was at 2:00 and I wanted it to be clean, even if it wasn't pristine. I had the top down when I picked up Melissa.

She had directions to Voxstall's place, and in a few miles, I began to have a hunch that we'd end up across from the junkyard. Sure enough, the guy who seemed to look through me when I sat in the junkyard was looking at me when we pulled up the long lane to his place. It was an old, restored two-story farm house, beautiful white clapboard siding with fresh paint, a gray wood porch surrounding the whole thing with wicker furniture scattered around. He had a couple blankets out in the yard, and some sort of classical music was playing in the background as we walked towards the place. I expected Martha Stewart to show up at any minute.

"This is my friend Bryce Hannon," Melissa said as she introduced me to Voxstall.

"Randy Voxstall," he said as he shook my hand. It was kind of a weak grip, like shaking hands with a ventriloquist's dummy. He was a tall guy, about 6' 4", a couple inches taller than me and it looked like he was about 50, an athletic build. He looked like a guy who thought a lot of himself. I couldn't help but wonder how a music Ph.D. had enough money for this horse farm.

Melissa saw a colleague over by the fence feeding a pretty dapple gray Arabian a carrot and Voxstall asked me if I cared for a drink. I did. But mostly I wanted him to tell me things that would help me understand what was going on across the road, and in the department.

He'd made a big batch of mint juleps, perfect for a party at a horse farm I thought. I took my tin cup full of crushed ice and poured some over the top. Nothing like a mint julep. Like an adult snow cone.

"I graduated from AU," I said. "How do you like the place?"

"I've only been here two years," he said. "We still have a lot of restructuring to do, and not everybody's going to be happy. But it can't be my goal to make everybody happy."

"Well, based on what I've heard, you probably stand a good chance of exceeding your goal," I said. He looked at me, and I could see he was unsure how to respond. I was enjoying his drink, I was enjoying his farm, I was enjoying his discomfort, and I was enjoying watching Melissa feed the horses. I decided if he wasn't going to talk, it must still be my turn.

"I was out here yesterday looking for parts for that old car I'm restoring. I think I saw a bunch of dogs running around. Boxers?" I said.

"I have three," he said. Three bitches and I hope to find a male to breed them with. I love breeding boxers. They're so excitable that I left them in the house for the picnic."

"A great dog," I agreed. "May I see them?"

He led me into the house. It was an old farm kitchen and the boxers were so enthusiastic about a visitor they almost knocked me over. I looked around. It was a classically renovated farmhouse. And on the counter was a white ceramic cat.

"You know, Melissa's boxer is missing."

"Yes, so I hear," he said. "Tragic. I hope it turns up."

"In fact," I said, "come to think of it, I'm sure I looked over after hearing that sound that must have been the shot that killed Butch Renninger and seeing three boxers chasing each other around on the porch, but not you. Were you around yesterday?"

"Are you a cop?" Voxstall said.

"No. Just a guy trying to fix up an old car," I said. "So were you around?"

He looked at me like he was trying to remember if his shotgun was loaded. "I can't remember," he said. "I should be a good host and go back outside," he said.

Of course," I said, and we went out onto the porch. "Butch told me yesterday that you weren't his biggest fan," I said.

"Mr. Renninger and I didn't agree on some land use issues," he said.

"Is that right?" I said. "And you killed him?" I asked, swallowing the julep in one gulp. "By the way, excellent mint julep. May I have a second cup?"

He refilled my tin mug with ice and poured the mint julep over the top. For some reason, he found it hard to stop pouring and the sweet brown elixir ended up overflowing my tin cup. The jaw muscles in his face were flexing rhythmically. It didn't seem like he was thinking about art appreciation at that very minute. "Mr. ... Hanson is it?" he said. "If you're doing this to be funny, or just for the shock value, you're failing miserably on both fronts. I have guests to attend to. And I think you may have worn out your welcome." He smiled. But not happily. "Have a nice afternoon."

I thought that went well.

Monday morning: I stopped at the office and told Dottie I'd be out doing some field work all morning. Naturally, there was no coffee. That is to say, there HAD been coffee, but I didn't get there before she drank it all.

"You get here on time some day, you might be surprised how much you'll enjoy it," she said.

"That would mean spending more time with you, Dottie. I'll have to decide if it's worth it," I said.

I had decided that I'd put my dad's old survey equipment to use with Mike McCarty. A land surveyor uses a transit, sometimes called a gun. It's like a tripod with a small telescope mounted on top. The telescope is calibrated and attached to show all 360 degrees of a circle around it. So a surveyor can set the transit up on a corner of a property and, based upon the angle of a corner, and using sine, cosine and tangent, establish the lines for the property. It's like a practical use for geometry. Imagine that. I had bought a couple of orange vests from the contractor supply store in Falls City a few months ago that almost always made a nosy property owner presume we were doing something official. Mike and I were going to pretend to be surveying Voxstall's neighbor's property that Monday morning. That way, we could watch both the junkyard and Renninger house, and now in a bonus, we could watch the Voxstall farm as well.

In a hollow behind the Voxstall house, as we were walking out to what appeared to be a corner of the property, I saw that there was a 200-yard target range, with targets set up at what looked like the 50-, 100- and 150-yard marks. Voxstall didn't strike me as the marksman type. But it looked like targets had been up, fresh, used by someone who knew what he was doing. Voxstall had somebody working in his barn. I saw a red Ford F-150 drive away from the barn, a guy in a cowboy hat. I put the gun on him. I didn't recognize him.

"You know what they say about cowboy hats and hemorrhoids," Mike said.

"What," I gave in.

"Sooner or later, every asshole has one."

Asshole drove down the lane and went across to the junkyard. I followed him with the gun. He knocked on Mary Jane Renninger's door and she opened it, and gave him the leash to a boxer. With a boxer on the other end. He led the boxer to the truck and brought him back up to the house. It appeared to me that J.R. was making a conjugal visit.

Mike and I snuck over to the barn while Asshole was in the house. It was a big old bank barn, glorious in its construction with an original slate roof that had been replaced with new slate – unheard of. That alone would cost $100 grand. For a roof. Something was up. Inside, there was a barn full of hay. Naturally. But this was a lot of hay. Two stories high, and about 50 feet in length and width, built against the back of the barn. For the dozen horses, this was … like a three-year supply. He wasn't making hay, and he wasn't selling hay, so a lot of this hay would get moldy before it could be used. Unless it wasn't all hay.

I told Mike to stand guard and walked over to check it out. Hay bales form enough of a grid that you can wind your way through them if you do it right. I built myself a tunnel, and worked my way back through the layers.

I guess I wasn't surprised to find the drugs. I was surprised to find the dogs.

I told Mike about the scene.

My guess was we were talking about 20-30 million dollars of drugs, based on what I saw stacked in the barn. It looked like it was coming to the barn in the middle of hay shipments, and Voxstall was bringing truckloads of hay from Mexico with drugs in the middle of every load. Turns out NAFTA was working after all.

As to the mill, there were probably 150 dogs, all sedated within an inch of their lives with trazadone. He probably got it from his horse vet and kept it on hand, using it in smaller doses for the dogs. He was running a big-time puppy mill and keeping the things starved and drugged until he bred them. Small cages stacked on top of each other, the things were basically barely alive. Boxers, collies, labs – the popular breeds. All of them had electric collars on to shock them if they barked. My guess is that he was selling 20 puppies a week, advertised as purebred, at $150 each, wholesaling them to pet stores. The wall of hay he'd built around the mill was built to absorb sound. He'd thought it out pretty well. No doubt, J. R. was actually Jack, Melissa's dog, used for his house breeding for now, destined for the mill after he'd done his work.

We were walking back, and I noticed a cop car going up to the Renninger house. Amy Gregson got out and I figured, good, maybe she was going back in to question Mrs. Renninger. We'd have more to talk about next time I saw her. Maybe our talk was worthwhile after all. Then she came out carrying two ceramic cats.

I was sure now that the game involved Amy, Mary Jane, and Voxstall, but I still wasn't sure who did what, other than Voxstall was importing drugs.

"Who shives a git if you don't have all the answers," Mike said. "You're in over your head, pal. This is DEA territory, or somebody like that, but it's not you, it's definitely not me, and it's clearly time for you to buy me lunch, anyway."

He had a point. I was hungry.

We stopped at McCleary's again because Mike said the Yankees were playing a businessman's special and the game would be on TV. He drank a beer and ate a burger and fries and I had a Cobb salad and a club soda.

"You should drink less, you know it, Mike? And this lunch – fried, fatty food. It's not good for you," I said.

"Thanks mom," Mike said. "You know there's a word for people who spend their days telling other people about their food choices."

"Yeah," I said. "It's called friendship."

"No," he said. "It's called none of your business. Let me know if you need me to help you find it in the dictionary. So what do you want to do about this?"

"You mean the Voxstall farm mess?"

"No, I mean David Cone as a starting pitcher. Yes, I mean the Voxstall farm, et al."

"I'm going out to Butch's trailer tonight to look around," I said.

"Let me just say," Mike said, "that you've had a lot of dumb ideas in your time, but I continue to be impressed at your ability to break new ground every day in terms of stupidity."

"Thank you," I said. "It's my competitive nature to want to be the best at something."

I drove back to the office. Dottie was gone for the day but she left me a note: "We were out of coffee so I bought more. You owe me $3.29. PS: Call Melissa Sherwood. She said it was important."

I dialed Melissa.

"Bryce," she said. "I'm not sure what happened yesterday at the party, but Voxstall has been positively a jerk to me all day.

"We had a conversation about a couple of things and I got the impression he was not enjoying my company," I said. "By the way, I'm pretty sure I found Jack."

I told her that I was still trying to put the pieces together but that I was within a day or two of being able to find Jack – that he was somewhere in the vicinity of the junkyard or Voxstall's farm. She wanted to go pick him up, but I convinced her that just showing up would blow a lot of cover. I said I was going out to the junkyard tonight and we would talk first thing in the morning and come up with a plan. She agreed but said she wanted to come along. I started to talk about it being dangerous and a bad idea, that these people were evil, and she said that we could talk about it on the way to the junkyard. I couldn't argue with that logic.

We drove to Butch's junkyard. Luckily it was a big moon – almost full – and I shut off my headlights for the last half-mile while we approached the yard. The gate to the yard had that yellow "Police Line: Do not cross" tape across it but it wasn't really what you'd call secure. I remembered that Butch kept the place locked but there were openings where the windows were, so I boosted Melissa up and she crawled in.

"Jackie boy!" she whispered. So we found Jack. I could hear a pretty happy reunion going on in there, and I hated to interrupt, but I needed to get inside.

"Ahem. Excuse me," I whispered, "but some of us are still on the outside looking in, here."

She let me in. The place was still cruddy, still bloody. No Butch. No cocaine. But the ledger book was still there. It was clear to me that Amy was all about making Butch a drug dealer, and drug dealers had no use for auto parts sales records. I took out my pen light and started looking through the ledger. The usual entries were there – "magnum 500 wheels, '70 Galaxie – 3 at $70 each." But I began to see a pattern of repeats "MJR – electronic ignition module '70 Duster – NC" followed by "MJR – electronic ignition module '73 Dart – NC." Beside the log book on the shelf was a half-dozen electronic control modules with the guts ripped out – little steel boxes that screwed open and shut. I thought of the rattle inside those ceramic cats.

And then Mary Jane Renninger turned on the lights in the little trailer.

"Well hello again, Mr. Hannon. The junkyard is closed," she said. "And, as you know, this is a crime scene. Perhaps you ought to come up to the house, and we'll telephone the police to talk about why you're here?"

She looked like she'd just come back from a dinner party, except she was carrying a .38 Special. So if she had been to dinner, maybe it was an NRA fundraiser or something. I remembered the old expression, "You can get more from a kind word and a gun than you can with a kind word."

So Melissa, Jack and I went to the spotless little rancher.

"Keep that dog under control," she warned as she opened the door. But it was too late. Jack knew what he was doing as soon as the door swung open. He was after that tuxedo cat like he had a date with destiny. The cat was jumping on counters, over couches, onto shelves, anywhere for protection. Jack followed him barking furiously. Mary Jane was yelling at him, and yelling at us, and then it seemed she realized she had a gun and started to level it at Jack.

The tuxedo cat jumped onto the island in the kitchen and Jack tried to jump up there, too, knocking over a ceramic cat in the process. It fell, shattered, and a black steel box lay before us. I gave a chop to Mary Jane's hand and the gun fell to the floor. I picked it up, and asked Melissa to grab Jack.

"Let's just open this box," I said to Mary Jane.

Just then, Amy Gregson opened the house door, accompanied by Randy Voxstall. I may not know everything, but I know that when a woman whom you used to date, who later turns out to be a drug dealer in league with a puppy mill operator and a conniving junkyard owner's widow, shows up at the home of the widow just as you are about to open a box of gold, it's going to be an interesting day.

"Bryce, what a pleasant surprise," Amy said with a twisted little smile. She had pulled her police issue 9 mm semiautomatic, and leveled it at me. And then, as if she could read my mind, she leveled it at Jack.

"Give me the gun, Bryce. I wouldn't want anyone or any dog to get hurt," she said, smiling again.

"Well, this is turning out to be a real party!" said Mary Jane. "'Not everyone can stay, unfortunately," said Voxstall. "I've got Chico outside, and he says he can operate the car crusher. Maybe your guests would like to see how it works."

I deduced that Chico was Asshole by another name, perhaps less apt, and I saw how this was going to work: Melissa and I in the Dart, crushed; Jack goes home with Voxstall; Amy and Mary Jane and Voxstall continue with business as usual. It pained me to think of the Dart crushed. The evening had definitely taken a menacing turn, and for a moment I considered whether, on the whole, Mike McCarty may have been right.

And then, what do you know, Mike shows up. With the State Police Narcotics Task Force. About a dozen cops with big guns and a megaphone and several black Chevy Suburbans. Chico wasn't going to be a problem after all.

Mike introduced me to State Police Lieutenant Shoffstall and I was ever so happy to tell him the whole story, with Mary Jane, Voxstall, and Amy agog.

Mary Jane would arrange for the drugs to be delivered to Voxstall's farm on tractor trailers, surrounded by hay. Amy distributed the drugs to dealers throughout Pennsylvania. Dealers would pay in cash, but in the late 1980s, after the whole "Just Say No" campaign, new regulations designed to stop the drug trade scrutinized any deposits greater than $10,000. So Mary Jane took the cash from Amy and traveled the mid-Atlantic, buying up pure gold jewelry with it. She would come back, open the clay cats, seal them up again, paint them, and melt down the gold jewelry inside the steel boxes. Mike had told me gold melts below the firing temperature of ceramics, and that steel melts above the firing temperature of ceramics. So the steel boxes neatly created 3x4 bars of gold which could be converted to cash less suspiciously, and as needed. The ceramic cats were a handy (albeit unusual) device to distribute the wealth to the participants in the scheme. I suggested that the Lieutenant check closets and basements for cats; and eventually 219 ceramic cats were recovered.

Amy had killed Butch Renninger, shooting him from the road after sighting in a deer rifle at Voxstall's farm earlier in the day. Then, Mary Jane detained me in her house with coffee long enough for Amy to get back to police headquarters and respond to the call. Jack, or "J.R." as Butch had called him, was scheduled to be taken by Chico up to the farm at the same time; thus he was gone by the time I found Butch dead.

Voxstall allowed his property and his trucks to be used for a cut of the action, and Amy made sure to look the other way on the puppy mills, so that he had additional revenue from that operation.

Butch was clean. He ran a junkyard. Mary Jane told him she wanted the Electronic Control Modules to melt down some jewelry, and he thought: fine. But the morning I heard them on the phone, something must have happened. I was guessing that Jack had knocked over *another* ceramic cat and Butch had become suspicious.

Epilogue

"Bryce, my boy," Mike said, "You gotta get yourself another car and quit hanging out at these junkyards. It's getting dangerous," he said over a beer later that evening.

I said that the car had nothing to do with it, and he should pay me for the Yankees bet he had lost on Friday.

"Pal, anybody who drives a car old enough to be placed in a car crusher without suspicion is asking for it," he said. "Buy yourself a Subaru or something."

"You may have something," I said. "I've been thinking of getting out of the old car game anyway."

"Really?!" Mike said.

"Yeah," I said. "I'm taking up yoga."

2016

The Float

Jonathan Richmond

Maybe the gods were plotting against me as I hit all sixteen red lights on Pulaski Highway or maybe they weren't. Pulaski Highway stretches all the way from the County to the City. In the County, Ikeas, Best Buys, and Chipotles line the road, and you know you reached the city when the consumer sprawl turns into by-the-hour-motels and liquor stores. As the malaise of the Great Recession of 2009 faded, much of Baltimore experienced a renaissance, but not this part of town. Under Armor isn't building here. I turned left into the parking lot of the Gentlemen's Gold Club. I wasn't there for a lap dance, rather business and a pit beef sandwich from Chaps, a dive that happened to share the same parking lot with one of Baltimore's finest jiggle-joints. I had a meeting with Larry Driskel, a divorce attorney, who lately hadn't called upon the services of my private investigation firm, Tarrou Security Services. Larry was in the line, which now wrapped around the small building. He waved me over to where he stood.

Larry was in his mid-fifties, with a round face and mustache like Tom Selleck's. He was short, overweight and wore a tan suit that highlighted his weeble-wobble frame. He only took cases of wives. Maybe he hoped he could be their rebound guy. We got our sandwiches -- heaps of beef, sausage, and American cheese, topped with "vegetables" from the questionably sanitary fixin' bar, smashed onto a sub roll too small for its contents -- and sat down at a small picnic table outside. Cars whizzed by on the highway while Larry slurped soda from his large white Styrofoam cup.

"I got a case for you," he said.

Larry's cases were typical of the divorce industrial complex. What would it be this time? Sitting in a seedy motel parking lot snapping photos of hubby with his mistress or uncovering dirt for a child custody battle? "Good to hear. My normal rates apply. Just like you shysters, I charge by the minute."

He half-smiled as if he were immune to jabs about his profession. "My client is Mrs. Molly Berger, wife of Ira Berger, owner of A-Plus Check Cashing. He's got fifteen stores in different locations throughout the Baltimore-Metro region."

Check-cashing joints are all over Baltimore, serving mostly poor city dwellers who have no relationship with a bank. A-Plus had a considerable market share, and I guess you could say Berger is the banker of the unbanked. "Fascinating," I said. "Tell me more boring shit."

"All right, Ben, don't be a dick." I was getting under his skin. Good. "Whenever I get a new client we do a financial background check to facilitate property and asset division. To make sure my client gets her due share."

"And yours, I'm sure," I added.

"I got two ex-wives of my own," he said. "Berger's all spread out. My financial guys finally tracked most of the business's accounts to two small thrifts -- Carrollton Savings and Loan, and Westminster Savings and Loan. That's where the money is supposed to be."

"Bank fraud?"

For the first time today, Larry had my attention.

He took out a thick manila folder from his briefcase and flopped it onto the picnic table. "Yeah, check-kiting. Here's the summary of the accounts from Carrollton and Westminster. My guys highlighted the discrepancies."

I studied the report for a few minutes. I'd worked some fraud cases before (for the insurance industrial complex), and Berger appeared to be running a circular scam. He was depositing bad checks written from his Carrollton account and then into the Westminster account. To cover the bad checks, he would write another bad check from his Westminster account and deposit it into his Carrollton account. Berger was taking advantage of the float – the time it takes between when the funds are "credited" and when the funds actually show up -- to inflate his balances and then make withdrawals with money that never existed. The scam is so pathetically simple, but I guess most scams are.

"Are the banks and cops aware of this yet?" I asked.

"Not yet. Carrollton and Westminster are up to their eyeballs in subprime trash and default swaps. We're thinking once they get a grip on their balance sheets, they'll realize Berger is another one of their toxic assets. Remember the Satisky brothers? They managed to run their kiting scam for over three years before they got caught, and shit, Bernie Madoff ran his Ponszi scheme right under the nose of the SEC for over three decades. If the markets didn't tank he'd probably still be in business. Let's not give our overlords too much credit."

How much?" Considering all the lime green highlights on the report, Berger was doing a number on the banks.

Larry nodded his fat head slowly. "My guys estimate Berger has been running the scam for almost two years. The losses for the bank are in the ballpark of ten million dollars. Berger's scheme probably would have been discovered if only the damn banks talked to each other."

Monday morning quarterbacking was right. Maybe if they had communicated this never would have happened. Isn't the communications revolution the mantra of the 21st century – WI-FI, 4G technology, Smart Phones, and IPads? For a connected world, there sure isn't a lot of communication, just hyper-chaos. The world was moving faster and the banks hadn't caught up yet. "So what is it exactly that you need me to do?"

Larry attempted to take another sip from his large cup, but it was empty. "Nobody's seen Berger for a week."

"So you want me to find him? Why not just call the FBI and let them find him?"

We need to find him before the banks or FBI figure out what's going on. Mrs. Berger is very concerned about her finances. Very concerned. Plus, you know how these well-to-do folks like to keep their dirty little secrets in the closet."

Larry sat and watched me as I considered his proposition. I was concerned about my finances too. The data manipulators at the Bureau of Labor and Statistics reported the economy was recovering, but the economy's long slump was still hurting business; insurance companies and lawyers weren't subcontracting private dicks as much as they once were. "I'll take the case."

Larry, satisfied with himself, took out another manila folder. He stood up and flipped the second folder on the table. "Here is some more background info on Mr. Berger. His wife is on a Caribbean cruise and will be back in a few days. I'll have her contact you when she gets back if Berger doesn't turn up by then. This should be enough information to get you started. I'm going to get a cocktail and a lap dance at the Gold Club. Want to come?" he asked lecherously.

I scoffed, "Can't; I'm working."

I sat at my desk and analyzed the contents of the two thick manila folders: a few photos of Berger, financial disclosures, a list of the A-Plus locations, and real estate reports, one of which listed both a house in Bethany Beach and a membership at the yacht club. My instincts, which had been off lately, told me Berger was alive and on the run.

How was he paying for things? He had easy access to cash, and attempting to track him via his debit and credit card transactions would lead me nowhere. Where is he sleeping? Berger might not need cash, but he certainly needed somewhere to sleep. My friends in the city and county police departments were checking the hotels and motels in the area for his black, 2012 Mercedes E350 sedan with vanity tags that read "CSHMNY". The beach house would be an obvious place not to hide if you were used to being on the run, but Berger was a businessman gone bad, and I hoped he would be dumb enough to go there.

I headed to slower-lower Delaware in my 2005 red Honda Civic; nothing fancy, but it's good on gas. To avoid the construction on the Bay Bridge, I headed north into Delaware then south to the beaches. Traffic on Coastal Highway was minimal. I passed through the beach party town of Dewey, then through the trailer-parks on Indian River Inlet, and finally into upscale Bethany Beach.

I turned onto Oceanview Parkway and onto Seabreeze Drive. Berger's house was the third on the right. The two-story house, with a white porch that wrapped around the entire second floor, was within walking distance to the beach, and he'd probably overpaid for it during the housing bubble. Berger's car wasn't in the driveway, and since it was early October, only one of the houses on the block appeared to be occupied. I wanted to take a look around. One can never be too careful, so I grabbed my Kahr nine millimeter out of the glove box. My carry permit wasn't any good in Delaware, but I'm not one for details, anyways. From the trunk, I grabbed a pizza warmer box that I bought off a Domino's delivery guy for fifty dollars about a year ago. I had used the box a few times as cover when doing surveillance, and my pizza-man disguise hadn't failed yet. I knocked on the door and rang the doorbell. No answer. I walked around the back and looked in the large bay windows. Nothing. Following the staircase to the second floor, I circumnavigated the porch, looking in each window. Zip. Satisfied he wasn't there, I thought maybe I was underestimating Berger's criminal mind. It was time to go. I was hungry for pizza.

As I walked down the stairs, a man approached. "Hey, what are you doing?"

I was about to find out if the fifty dollars for the pizza box was worth it. "Somebody ordered a pizza to this address, but no one is home."

"Nobody has been there for over a year," the man said.

"This isn't the Horowitz residence?" I asked.

No, this is the Berger residence, and they haven't been here in over a year."

"This is 221 Seabreeze Drive, isn't it? Are you sure this isn't the Horowitz residence?"

"Yes, I'm sure." He was getting annoyed. I think my snooping was making him late for his tee time. "And I should know, I'm here all year round." He wasn't completely convinced I was a pizza delivery man. It was time to go.

"God darn it! Somebody must be making prank calls again. You know, a man tries to make a living, and he has to deal with this shit. I better be going before these other pizzas get cold."

I hopped in my car and sped off. In my rearview mirror, I saw the man turn and walk back to his house. Domino's does deliver.

The Bethany Yacht Club was a five-minute drive from Berger's house. At the entrance was a gate and security hut. Rich people sure do go out of their way to keep the unworthy out of their clubs. The security hut was empty. In the off-season, the gate was probably sufficient to keep undesirables out. I pulled up to the callbox and mashed all the buttons. The gate buzzed and then opened slowly.

I entered the grounds and parked my car near the large club house. As I walked to his boat, I thought how most of these cost more than three times as much as my townhouse. A man sat on a boat next to Berger's. He was middle-aged, with coffee-color skin, most likely from days on the water. He was drinking a Heineken and smoking a cigarette.

"Hi there." I stuck out my hand. "I'm Ben. I'm here to look at the boat for sale. Is this Ira Berger's boat?"

"Nick Marino." He hesitantly shook my hand. "I didn't realize he was selling it."

I examined the boat, pretending to know what I was looking at. The bow had a large teak deck, a polished brass handrail that followed the length of the starboard and port, and two fighting chairs on the stern. Through the windows, I could see the cabin was flush with amenities: the salon featured an entertainment center with two-large flat-screens, a full bar, and two leather couches. I couldn't see inside the master or guest staterooms, but I had a feeling they were just as posh. "What would you pay for a boat like this?"

A 46-foot Hatteras Convertible. Let's see, I would think in this condition," he tapped his chin with his finger and looked up as if he this were the most perplexing question he had been asked in awhile. "About a hundred fifty thousand. If he really wants to get rid of it, maybe one and a quarter."

Trying not to be obvious about my real intentions for being there, I engaged Nick in some small talk about the boat, fishing, and places we'd seen. He seemed to enjoy my company, and I was enjoying his. I finished being subtle and asked, "What can you tell me about Mr. Berger, so I know what to offer him for the boat?"

"I haven't seen him or his wife in awhile, but they weren't my kind of people. They were all about making sure everybody knew they had money. Typical of the people around here. The only thing most of them know about boats is that they float. Me, I just want to be on the water. I don't give a shit who knows I have money. Plus, I drink too much and I smoke too much. I guess you could say I'm the club pariah."

I knew what it was like to be an outsider in an unreasonable world. I gave an understanding smile. "When's the last time you saw Mr. Berger on the boat?"

He lit a cigarette and grabbed another Heineken out of his cooler. "Last time I saw Ira was over a year ago at the Labor Day social. You want a beer?"

I drank a beer with Nick and even smoked my first cigarette in twenty years. It tasted like shit, but I still found it soothing. I could have sat on his boat all day, but I had a job to do. I finished my beer; Nick cracked another; we shook hands again, and I walked back to my car. I had a feeling Nick knew I wasn't really interested in the boat; my commonness was all too evident. I headed back to Baltimore, no closer to finding Berger.

I went back to my office. Bethany had been a bust, and none of my contacts had a word on Berger's Mercedes. I grabbed the list of A-Plus locations off my desk and headed out to see if I could get any information. The first three stores yielded little information. All the employees I talked to knew nothing about Berger. To them, he was just the man who signed their paychecks.

Finding Berger was proving to be more difficult than I had originally anticipated. I carried on-- only eleven more stores to go. The fourth store was across the street from Lexington Market. The smell of chitlins (imagine hot garbage) polluted the air. In front of the market, several men stood eating fried chicken, wiping their greasy mouths with slices of white bread. The inside of the store was a large rectangle, with a long U-shaped wall of bulletproof glass running the perimeter of the store. Rich people used gates to keep the riffraff out whereas on the mean streets of Baltimore, bulletproof glass was the preferred deterrent. Behind the glass, in front of a register, a forty-five-millimeter pistol and an aluminum baseball bat were visible, a warning to anyone who thought about doing something crazy. On my right, a large neon "Lottery" sign hung above two black girls operating the number machines. To the left stood a walk-in cooler filled with malt liquor and back-alley champagne. In the middle of the store were three rows of shelves, half-filled with cheap cleaning products, toiletries, and knock-off Hallmark sympathy cards. Towards the back, customers cashed checks, paid bills, and filled out Western Union forms on the counter ledge. The store reminded me of a casino where the cash cages were located in the back, making it impossible to leave without passing the bar, gaming tables, or slot machines. I approached one of the young black girls working the lottery machine. "Hey, I'm Ben. I work for *The Baltimore Sun*, and I was wondering if I could speak to a manager."

She didn't say anything and headed towards the check cashing cage to talk to a white girl who was helping customers. She followed the lottery girl back to me. The white girl was probably in her late twenties or early thirties, with a pallid complexion and fake hair tied in a long ponytail. She was dumpy, had a diamond stud in her right nostril, and a tattoo on her flabby right arm of the comedy/tragedy masks with the message "Laugh Now, Cry Later, Bitch." She looked tough but was obviously letting her guard down, excited about meeting a "real" reporter. Over the years I realized that those on the margins of society refuse to talk to the police or anyone remotely linked to law enforcement, but were more than willing to talk to a reporter. When you are used to being ignored all your life, you'll talk to anyone who might be able to get your story out.

She flipped her hair to the side and said, "Hi, Hon. I'm Ms. Honey, the manager. What can I do for youz, Hon?"

"I'm Ben Tarrou from *The Sun* paper." I stuck out my hand. Ms. Honey extended her hand high, fingers pointed downwards, as if we were in the 19th century. I shook her fingers and hoped she didn't expect me to kiss her hand. "I'm doing a story on the check cashing business. Could I ask you a few questions?"

"Oh my, I've never been interviewed before. Let me get my cigarettes, and we'll go outside and talk, okay, Hon?"

Outside she lit a cigarette and offered me one. For the second day in a row, I was smoking. This coffin nail tasted better than yesterday's and gave me a buzz. Taking out a small notepad and a pen, I started the interview with some questions about Ms. Honey, playing to her desperate desire to be important.

"My real name is Ella Nesbit, but all the regulars call me Ms. Honey. Before I started working here, I would always buy honey-flavored blunts. I was here so often, Ira, my boss, gave me a job."

Evidently, Berger had no problem hiring potheads. Pretending to take notes, I scribbled gibberish in my notepad.

"How long have you worked here?"

"Almost ten years, Hon," she said proudly.

At least Berger hired reliable potheads. "You the only manager?"

She lit another cigarette with the first one. "Uh-huh. When I started, I was just a lottery girl. Ira used to run the store, but he's way too busy these days, so he promoted me to manager. Are you going to take my picture?"

"Maybe. Do you like being manager?"

"I sure do, Hon. I know all the regulars; I know their lucky numbers, where they work, what they drink. It's like one big ghetto family." She laughed, amused at herself.

"That's cute." I sarcastically smiled, which, of course, she thought was sincere.

"On the other hand, Ira's been a real bitch lately. He could pay me a little better and treat me with some respect. I know he thinks I'm just a dumb white bitch from Pigtown, but it wasn't for me this place would be a bigger shithole than it already is. He was going to make me general manager of the new store in Woodlawn, but he put the move on hold when the regression started. I tried to talk to him about the new store a month ago and he told me that I should be happy I had a job at all."

I gave a confused look. "Regression? Do you mean recession?"

She batted her eyes, shrugged her shoulders, and gave an innocent look. "Silly me, Hon. Yeah, recession."

I didn't remember any mention of a store in Woodlawn in the report. Could I have missed it? "Where exactly is this store?"

"In the Meadow Park Shopping Center, right off Security. He's spent a lot of his time there since he and his wife separated. Putting the store on hold was a real disappointment. Now the store is just like most of the other stores in Meadow Park – empty."

I wrote down the address and put the notepad back in my pocket. "Thanks a lot, Ms. Honey. I think I got enough."

"That's it?" she said, disappointed. No one had listened to her for a long time, and now I was leaving. "When is the story going to be in the paper?"

"I'm not sure exactly. I just do the interviews. It was nice meeting you, Ms. Honey." Feeling somewhat bad for taking advantage of her naïveté, I slipped her a twenty.

I left the city and headed into the county. Thanks to Ms. Honey, I had my first break. In this business, sometimes it's better to be lucky than good. But how could I have missed the Woodlawn store? I recalled a TV show about a Virginia lawyer who was busted hiding assets from his ex-wife. The Arlington lawyer gave some of the legal fees he had earned to his mother, and she put the cash in an account in her name. The plan was for her to give the money to him after the divorce was final. Eventually, he was caught and lost his attorney's license. Was it possible Berger was doing the same thing? Had he purchased the Woodlawn store after his wife had filed for divorce, and put the store in someone else's name? Berger was turning out to be one sneaky son of a bitch.

I drove east on the Beltway, storm clouds rolled in, and rain pattered on my windshield. Despite the worsening weather, which usually ensures gridlock around Baltimore, there was little traffic. My cell phone vibrated in my pocket; it was Larry.

"What's up, Larry? I'm in the county. Did you know Berger was opening a store in Woodlawn?"

"No clue. Are you sure?"

"I'm about to find out."

"Well, you better find out fast. I just got a call from Carrollton Savings and Loan, and Berger's gig is up. The FBI is involved and they're looking for him too."

"Good to know," I said. "I'll call you when I know something."

I exited off the Beltway, drove east on Security Boulevard, and took a right into the Meadow Park Shopping Center. The western section of the shopping center housed a grocery store, a dry cleaners', and a Subway; the three stores in the eastern section were vacant. Two of the three stores had "For Lease" signs on their windows. I pulled around back, and there was Berger's Mercedes. CHSMNY! I parked the car, and, remembering the guns on display in Berger's stores, I grabbed mine out of the glove compartment.

At the back door, I grabbed the knob, and the door opened. "Berger, you in there?" No answer. The inside was dark, and cigarette smoke staled the air. A few tools, work benches, and planks of wood lay scattered on the floor. In the back, another door led to an office where a faint light beamed from the bottom of the door. I headed to the back, took out my gun, and cautiously entered the office.

The office was bare, except for a half-empty water cooler to my left and a desk in front of me. Empty bottles of Christian Brothers' brandy and cigarette butts were scattered across the floor. I walked around the back of the desk, and there Berger lay in the fetal position. His clothes were filthy and he'd probably been wearing the same outfit since he went missing. A gray, scraggly beard had taken over his firm narrow face. I bent down, put two fingers on Berger's scruffy neck, checking for a pulse, nearly gagging at the reek of his breath. He was alive, just wasted. I checked him for weapons, but he was clean. I took the large blue cooler off its stand and dumped the water onto Berger's face and torso. Sputtering, he jumped up, stumbled, and fell back into the wall.

"What the fuuu," he slurred.

"You're a tough man to find, Berger."

"Who the fuck are you?"

"Now, now. No need to be vulgar. Ben Tarrou, private investigator. I was hired by your wife's lawyer to find you." Berger stumbled and pulled himself onto the desk chair and sat. He was soaking wet; the water cooler shower was probably the closest thing to a bath he'd had in more than a week. His hands reached for the desk drawer. I pointed my gun at him. "Easy there, cowboy. Let's not do anything stupid."

He put his hands in the air. "Just getting something to drink and smoke. If that's okay with you, Mr. Private Investigator." He sneered and was struggling to keep his hands up.

I nodded for him to continue, watching his every move, ready to use my gun to erase his face. At the same time I hoped violence wouldn't be necessary. Berger pulled a new bottle of brandy out of his bottom drawer and slammed it unintentionally on the desk. He struggled to open the bottle. Finally getting it opened, he took a large swig of the brown firewater and then lit a cigarette.

"Lots of people looking for you. Including the FBI."

Berger took another long pull of brandy. He grimaced. "I've been waiting. Didn't think a private investigator would be looking for me, but the FBI, I knew it was only a matter of time. Should have known that bitch would have sent someone looking for me. She's probably worried about her money or her fucking social status. That's all she ever carried about – money. Boy, is she in for a surprise." He smiled wickedly.

Like he was in a clichéd detective novel where the villain meets his demise, Berger wanted to tell his story. He wasn't on the run after all; he wanted to be found. "Why'd you do it? Is the check-cashing business that bad these days?"

"Are all private investigators smartasses?" His stoned eyes met mine.

"Most of us," I quipped back. He lit another cigarette and offered me one. I declined.

He rocked in his chair and tried again to find his equilibrium. "When I first met Molly, she was a bitch – and she still is. But I was young, stupid, and had confused good sex with love." He breathed heavily out of his nose. He was growling. "That cunt. We started with shit, but even when my business took off, nothing was good enough for her. We traveled, bought a beach house, a boat, went to all the great parties; she loved being part of the social scene." He ground his teeth and bit his lip; foam caked the corners of his mouth. "In the early part of the decade, I began to expand. Opening new stores, buying up real estate, then the housing bubble burst, and I knew I was in trouble. Things were going to have to change, but Molly didn't want to hear it. I started small, using the float to cover checks. I'd pay this bill or that bill, and then sling a check to cover it.: nobody even noticed. A thousand here, ten thousand there, and before I knew it I was in deep. The bankers, the ones who thumbed their noses at me and my business, were too busy running their own scams to even notice -- Freddie and Fannie, the real estate agents, the mortgage brokers, Wall Street bankers with their fancy financial instruments, all of them as guilty as I. You know, I once saw a mortgage broker authorize a four hundred thousand mortgage for someone with a three hundred fico score. Three fucking hundred. Dipshit shouldn't have been able to get a loan for a cold drink." He lit another cigarette; the tobacco sparkled, fueled by his combustible breath. "I knew it was over – my marriage and the scam. And the real kick in the ass was when Molly called me a loser who couldn't even take care of his family. What family? Molly ain't family. She's a hooker I rent for parties." He slammed his fist on the desk, then started laughing deliriously. "My life is a lie."

He reached into the bottom drawer of his desk again and pulled out a gun, a forty-five caliber. I raised mine, but he wasn't aiming for me. The float had gotten the best of Berger -- Molly, the Mercedes, the beach house, the boat, A-Plus, the parties, all of it – one big lie. He could no longer rely on the float; for him it was time for a reality check.

He put the forty-five in his mouth. I heard the barrel clatter against his teeth and he pulled the trigger. Nothing happened.

"The safety's still on," I said.

He took the gun out of his mouth, and searched for the safety release. Before he had a chance to find it I smacked the gun out of his hand and it slid across the floor away from Berger. Berger put his hands to his face and whimpered, "I can't even kill myself."

I picked up the gun, emptied the clip, jacked the slide to get the bullet out of the chamber, and left Berger. Then I called Driskel and 911.

I went outside and waited for Driskel and the police. My job was done, but I couldn't get what Berger said out of my head: all our lives are lies. Molly, Berger, the bankers, everyone buying time in the float – till the bills come due. Me, I'm no different; except I know there is nothing in my account.

2012

Out at Home

Chris Panzarella

Rooting for a baseball team as bad as the Edge City BayHawks is like being stuck in an abusive relationship. Every year they break your heart and embarrass you in public, but come spring you're right back in the bleachers rooting for them to win.

This kind of resiliency comes in handy *all* the time in my line of work. When you choose to work as a private detective you have to accept the fact that you are going to get the short end of the stick. A lot. Clients will refuse to pay, leads will refuse to pan out, and suspects will refuse to tip their hand. The list goes on.

However, every once in a great while, if he's lucky, a private detective will get a chance at a Big Case. The type where someone rich and famous has been murdered, assaulted, or otherwise brutally victimized in a criminal fashion. A case where everyone follows the news waiting to see what happens next. So naturally when a Big Case strolled into my office one humid July afternoon I was immediately suspicious.

* * * * *

My office, Mark Nelson Investigations, sits on West 19th street just a couple of blocks past a wonderful old blue collar neighborhood, recently renovated and now infested with yuppies. It occupies the second floor of a squat brick building sandwiched between a Chinese take-out joint and a squadron of shabby rowhouses.

I was sitting at my desk, an old mahogany monstrosity, listening to the BayHawks radio broadcast bounce off the warped walnut paneling that lined the walls when the door opened and a woman calmly walked in.

She wore a simple yet elegantly tailored navy blue suit and enough jewelry to be considered tasteful but not quite garish. A slim golden chain glimmered at her throat while a ring set with three sapphires sparkled on her left hand. Her outfit told me she was rich, rich enough to prefer discretion over attention. She glanced once around my office with an air of slight bemusement, took a seat on one of the plastic chairs I had picked up at Good Will for a buck, and cleared her throat.

"Mark Nelson?"

"Yes ma'am, what can I do for you?"

"My husband died last night."

I blinked. The woman didn't. She kept on talking. "I believe he was murdered, I want you to find out who killed him."

I coughed to buy a moment. "If this is a homicide case, and it certainly sounds like one, you need to call the police. Try Detective Lieutenant Portman at-"

The woman cut me short by shaking her head, slowly but firmly.

"No. I considered going to the police, but after they were implicated in the death of that young Hispanic boy I decided they couldn't be trusted. Besides, someone called them in already. They're checking out the crime scene as we speak."

I leaned back in my chair and looked at the woman questioningly. "If the police are already involved, why are you coming to me? What do you think I can do that they can't?"

"Like I said, I don't trust the police. I want someone independent looking at the evidence, someone who won't jump to an easy conclusion to satisfy the press."

I sighed, settled back into my chair and pulled out my notepad.

"Well, it looks like I'm your man then. Let's start at the beginning. What's your name?"

"Michelle Peterson. My husband was a local businessman named Arthur."

I paused and looked up.

"Arthur Peterson."

"Yes."

"As in Arthur Peterson, *owner* of the Edge City BayHawks."

"That's correct."

"Mrs. Peterson, I'm sorry to be the one to tell you this, but the list of people who hated your husband would stretch from my office into the next state. Do you follow baseball much?"

"Not particularly, no."

"Then you may not know that the BayHawks last put together a winning season three presidents ago. Players, coaches, managers, and even general managers have come and gone, but Mr. Peterson has presided over all of them. He is generally regarded as the biggest cause of the BayHawks' downfall. Trying to find his murderer will be like looking for a needle in a haystack made of needles."

Mrs. Peterson looked me right in the eye.

"Mr. Nelson, I appreciate your concerns. Would triple your normal rate be sufficient to allay them?"

I made a quiet choking sound. After a moment, I recovered.

"Okay, okay. I'll take the job."

"Excellent."

"One last question, though. This case is going to be a huge story. Why come to a small-timer like me?"

Mrs. Peterson presented her immaculate white teeth in an icy smile. "Because, Mister Nelson, I know all about your past. I know who you used to be. I imagine you will come into contact with all types of baseball-affiliated people in the course of your investigation. A man of your background should serve admirably in handling a situation such as this."

Now it was my turn to stare.

"Not many people know that I used to play for the BayHawks, especially since I took steps to change my name."

She lifted one hand in a gesture of apology. "In any case, I took the liberty of bringing my late husband's datebook with me. Feel free to peruse it at your leisure, but I must insist that you not write in the book and return it to me when finished."

She stood up and handed me an embossed business card.

"Here's my number; please contact me with any results. I wish you luck in your search."

With that she strode out of my office and shut the door behind her.

I put some water on for coffee and looked at the late Mr. Peterson's planner. It was bound in heavy red leather. I opened the front cover and started reading.

Arthur Peterson kept busy for a man of his advanced age. His schedule was crammed with business conferences, personal lunches with old friends, and committee meetings on the BayHawks' current affairs. After sifting through the last two months' worth of appointments I had a list of names but no obvious connections. I decided to take a break and stretch my legs. The All-Star game kicked off tomorrow in St. Louis. What better time to check out a murder scene?

* * * * *

I parked my beat-up old Ford three blocks over from Main Street and enjoyed a rare cool breeze on the afternoon summer air as I walked to my destination.

The BayHawks had played in Edge City Municipal Stadium since they moved here 45 years ago. Dubbed 'The Nest' by the locals almost immediately, it still brought to mind the grand old ballparks from the sixties, where the last of the Silver Age greats played out their careers. I flashed my ID card and detective's license at a side gate and was promptly waved through. Mrs. Peterson had apparently made sure I wouldn't have any trouble getting in to take a look around.

I stepped into the main concourse and took a slow, deep breath. Sometimes when I go to a game I'll just buy a beer and wander through the concourse, lost in a human sea of crackerjacks and conversation. This time, as I passed under the green steel archways, only wails of regret and whispers of ghosts long forgotten rose to meet me.

One of the park attendants, a pale, thin man with a paler, thinner mustache, unlocked the outfield gates and let me onto the field. I paused for a moment to crouch down and run my hands across a patch of outfield grass, savoring the texture, then continued on to meet the first challenge of the day. Several uniformed police officers stood guard over the infield dirt, their burnished shields glinting in the sunlight. Just past them a couple of crime scene technicians in dark blue windbreakers scurried around like fleas that had just caught the scent of blood. Unfortunately that scent was literal in this case. One of the officers held up his hand as I approached.

"Sir, this place is absolutely off limits to civilians, I'm going to have to ask you to leave immediately."

I shook my head and flashed my ID again. "Sorry, but I can't do that. I'm a private detective hired and retained by the Peterson estate. I need to take a look around."

The cop narrowed his eyes. "Perhaps you didn't hear me correctly sir. This scene is off-limits to civilians, and that especially includes a pathetic broken down old man pretending to be a-"

"Eddie, you're going to have to let him through."

We both looked at the speaker, a thirtyish man in a rumpled suit with brown hair and lines in his face. A detective's badge hung from the breast pocket of his suit.

Eddie sputtered. "Sir, you can't seriously be suggesting-"

Detective Lieutenant John Portman raised a hand. "Much as it pains me to admit it, Mr. Nelson appears to have friends in high places. I just got a call from Captain Reynolds; apparently we are to allow Mr. Nelson an unobstructed look at the scene." He stabbed a finger at me with a grimace. "You have five minutes, make the most of them. Don't touch anything or I'll haul you in on obstruction."

I simply nodded at Portman and made my way to home plate, conscious that the rest of the officers were watching my every move. When I reached my destination I just stood and took in the scene for a long moment.

Arthur Peterson hadn't died cleanly. His body lay face-up at home plate, his arms and legs skewed at angles that gave him the appearance of a drunken scarecrow. The left side of his face had been bludgeoned into a bloody ruin. I knelt down in the third base batter's box to get a closer look at his head. The left temple had completely caved in, but something seemed to have left a faint impression in the wound. The impression looked like something familiar. It looked like a baseball.

I stood up and walked back to the mound, taking care to avoid the crime scene techs who were snapping pictures and taking samples. Toeing the rubber, I took up a set position and stared in at home plate, thinking. The sounds of police chatter faded into the background as I focused my attention. From here Peterson was just a pinch hitter making the last appearance of his career. In my experience, things were always easier to sort out from a pitcher's mound. Unfortunately, this mound was behind on its maintenance; a couple of dirt clumps had been gouged out of each side.

I thought about the situation for a couple of minutes, then nodded to myself. The list of suspects had just gotten a lot shorter.

My five minutes were up. I bade farewell to Portman and his stable of uniforms and made my way back to the outfield gates.

* * * * *

I was walking back through The Nest's concourse when a large blond man came huffing up. Sweat glistened in sideburns wrought like golden wire. The man pulled off his large plastic eyeglasses, mapped his broad forehead with a white handkerchief, then stuck out his hand.

"Pleased to meet'cha sir. Miss Peterson said you'd be droppin' by. Name's Charlie Milton; I'm the equipment manager for the home team clubhouse at the stadium. Anythin' I can do to lend a hand?"

I glanced back the way I had come. "Now that you mention it, a question has occurred to me. How come the body hasn't been taken away yet? Have you talked to the police here at all?"

Charlie shook his head. "I don' really trust cops, not since some fat sergeant from the 3rd precinct ran my brother in on some bullshit fraud charges a couple years back. As for the body, given how high profile this crime's gonna be, I'd bet dollars to doughnuts they're takin' their sweet time to make sure they don't miss anything."

I sighed. "I can't say I'm surprised." I looked back at Charlie. "Come to think of it, there might be something you can do to help."

I took out the list of names I had copied from Peterson's date book and handed it over.

"Do you know where I can find any of these guys?"

Charlie slowly perused the list. After a moment he brightened. "Yeah, I can help ya out. The 'Hawks just got back from a long road trip. They've got the next couple 'o days off on account of the All-Star game and whatnot, but they start up again in three days. I know where ya can find a couple of these guys. Graham is still livin' with his parents up on

23rd street, and last I heard of ol' Crowley he was spending most of his days at the Edge City Library over on Cold River Way. They're the only two locals on this here list."

He handed the paper back to me and I folded it into an outside pocket of my jeans.

"You seem to know a great deal for a clubhouse manager."

Charlie shrugged. "I sometimes end up running errands for the guys. Plus, I feel like I can trust ya. Ya walk like a baseball player."

I thanked Charlie and walked back to my car.

* * * * *

I parked on east 23rd street and walked towards the residence of Mr. and Mrs. Graham. Their son Marty had been drafted out of high school by the BayHawks in the sixth round of the Amateur Draft. A promising infield prospect, he had risen steadily through the farm system. Two years ago he cracked the 'Hawks' major league roster as the starting third baseman and hadn't looked back since. His hitting skills were alternately described as adequate and a work in progress. Defensively, however, he was already drawing comparisons to the legendary Brooks Robinson, who had manned the hot corner up in Baltimore many years ago.

I knocked on the front door and Marty himself answered. A tall, rangy youth with clear green eyes, his posture spoke of an easy, self-confident grace. He looked me up and down.

"Sorry, we don't give out donations."

I smiled. "Thanks, but I'm not collecting. My name's Mark Nelson, I'm a private investigator. Do you have a minute to talk?"

Marty cocked his head slightly to one side. "What's this about?"

"Something serious has happened. I think it would be better if we talked about this indoors."

Marty narrowed his eyes. "Is there any particular reason I should trust you?"

I spread my hands. "Honestly? Not really."

Marty nodded slowly. "Sure, come on in, the parents are out to dinner."

The Graham household was well worn but comfortably lived in. Most of the furniture and decorations looked to be at least thirty years old but well cared for. Marty led me to the dining room table and sat down, motioning to the chair across from him. "So, what 'serious' matter are you investigating?"

I took out my notepad and watched Graham carefully. "Someone murdered Arthur Peterson last night."

I expected surprise, maybe a little shock. Instead the young third baseman merely nodded his head.

"I know, the manager told us this morning. The team is trying to keep the story out of the press, but they wanted the players to know firsthand."

I raised an eyebrow. "You seem pretty calm talking about death for someone your age."

Marty spread his hands with the palms up. "I'm not going to lie to you, death shouldn't be a cause for celebration. However, I really didn't care for that crotchety old bastard." He paused. "This conversation is off the record, right?"

I nodded. "Of course. There's no love lost between me and the Edge City press, don't worry. Getting back to Peterson, why didn't you like him?"

Marty scowled at the table. "Four years ago, I was ready for the major leagues. My manager at Triple-A knew it. The coaches there knew it. Even the other players knew it. Everyone knew it. Everyone, that is, except for Old Man Peterson. He saw the talent I had, but he didn't want to have to pay for it. So, he buried me.

"I toiled in the minor leagues for two more years until I finally forced them to put me on the major league roster. Who knows what those two lost years will do to my career?"

He took a deep breath and unclenched his hands. I looked at him, not unsympathetically. "Did the team officials tell you how Peterson died?"

Marty shook his head. "No, they didn't have any specifics."

"He was killed by a baseball to the head."

Marty looked up at me. "And you think I had something to do with it?"

"I wasn't going to put it that bluntly, but yes. While we're on the subject, can you tell me where you were last night?"

Marty narrowed his eyes. "The entire team flew in yesterday evening, except for Mel Hendricks, who's our representative at the All-Star game this year. I went out by myself for dinner and a couple of drinks then came home and went to sleep, but I can't prove any of it. On that note, I think it's time you left."

I didn't press the issue with him. It had been a long day.

* * * * *

As I rounded the corner back onto East 23rd the glow of a streetlamp revealed Portman's hunched figure sitting on my hood.

I stopped five feet away and kept my hands in view. "Good evening Detective Lieutenant, to what do I owe the pleasure?"

The man glanced up at me. "Spare me the pleasantries. You talked to some people today. People who don't talk to the police. What did they tell you?"

I shrugged. "Home gardening tips, mostly."

Portman scowled. "Stop fucking around, Nelson. My men are finishing with the crime scene as we speak. The only things I need now are witnesses. I know you're following up on a lead with Graham. Bring me into the loop and I won't make you regret it."

I shook my head slowly. "Sorry, I answer to Mrs. Peterson on this, if you can get her approval I'll tell you everything. You're welcome to arrest me if you want, but something tells me you need to move fast on this case and my being behind bars won't help you."

The detective looked at me long and hard, then threw up his hands as he got off my car. "Take one of my cards, it has my number. Damn it Nelson, we're on the same team here."

"With all due respect I play by a different definition of the word. Have a good night, Detective."

Portman's figure cast a long silhouette as I started my engine and drove off into the night.

I went home and poured myself a nightcap. As I sipped the whiskey I listened to a news broadcast covering an ongoing citywide strike by the municipal trash collectors as it crackled through my radio. According to the latest reports negotiations had picked up between city officials and the various union reps. Apparently the large buildups of garbage on street corners had sparked a public outcry to have the matter settled. Meanwhile, my case was still very much up in the air.

* * * * *

The next morning I scrambled two eggs to go with some toast and orange juice and ate quickly. I wanted to get to the Edge City Library before it opened.

Without a doubt, stakeouts are one of the most tedious aspects of being a detective. I parked the Ford across the street from the library's front doors and settled down to wait. Since I was stationed up the street I had a good view of people approaching the library from both directions.

During the first three hours I didn't have any luck. A pair of young mothers walked in together with their children. An hour and twenty minutes later, three older gentlemen in military veteran jackets trooped through the entrance, chatting quietly among themselves. Remarkably, a gaggle of adolescent kids crowded through the doors a short time later. I blinked at them in surprise; most people my age don't expect children to visit the library of their own free will these days. Finally, halfway through hour number five, my patience paid off.

Like countless BayHawk Fans I had seen Bud Crowley's face on TV often enough to be able to pick him out of a police lineup. Even in retirement his fluffy gray hair and thick, ruddy face hadn't changed much. It was easy to spot the man ambling down the sidewalk in the exact same gait he had used whenever he needed to walk onto the diamond and confront an umpire or two on a bad call.

I waited until he passed my car, then got out and crossed the street behind him. I entered the library four steps on this tail, scanned my library card at the front desk a few seconds after Crowley did, then held back and kept him within eyesight as he made his way to the Classics section. He went immediately to one high shelf, removed a book, and headed for a corner table. I gave him a minute to get comfortable, then approached.

"Bud Crowley?"

He looked up at me, then squinted after a moment.

"Do I know you, young man?"

I quickly shook my head. "No sir, my name is Mark Nelson. I'm a private detective investigating a murder."

"Is that so? Whose murder?"

"Arthur Peterson."

The weathered ex-manager studied my face for several long moments. Then he slowly closed his book. The man had been reading *Paradise Lost*.

"I think perhaps you should start from the beginning, young man."

I pulled up a chair and gave Crowley the condensed version of yesterday's events. When I was finished he rubbed the bridge of his bony nose with a broad thumb and forefinger.

"Given the circumstances, I assume you are here to question me?"

I nodded. Crowley sighed. "Young man, I managed the BayHawks for twelve years. Arthur Peterson was anything but a hands off owner during that time despite whatever he said in his daily press conferences. I doubt a single week went by without his finding some excuse to question my management of the team. The day I handed him my resignation was one of the most satisfying of my baseball career.

"We feuded constantly, I won't deny that. However, I do deny having a role in that man's death; it was far easier just to walk away. Besides, do you really think I could throw a baseball hard enough to kill at my age?"

I blinked. "I take it Marty Graham talked to you then."

"Indeed, he called me late last night, just after he spoke to you."

"In that case, I have just one other question. What did you and Marty talk about when the two of you had dinner with Mr. Peterson two weeks ago?"

This time it was Crowley's turn to blink. "How did you hear about that?"

"I have his datebook, he had a dinner scheduled with you and Marty Graham. So, what did the three of you talk about?"

He hesitated, but only for a moment. "We spoke of the future. Marty and I had each invested a considerable sum of money in a stock portfolio Arthur had set up. When the stocks tanked, we both wanted to cash out and cut our losses. The three of us met over dinner to discuss the particulars."

A wistful smile played across his weathered face. "I also asked about coming to spring training to throw some batting practice. Peterson turned me down; he had just bought two machines that can pitch to batters at speeds ranging from batting practice to over one hundred miles an hour."

I shook my head. "That's a bit of a shame. I always thought baseball was the last place for machinery like that."

Crowley nodded. "Besides that, I heard any time you set one up on a pitcher's mound it has a tendency to gouge out large chunks of dirt from it."

An image from The Nest crashed its way into my mind and a chill ran down my spine. I jerked out of the chair. "I have to go. Now."

Crowley smiled. "Sure. It was nice seeing you again, Billy."

I had already started to walk away, but stopped dead in my tracks at those words. I turned back to my ex-manager.

"I...hoped that you had forgotten about me after so many years."

He shook his head. "Not a chance, but don't worry. Your secret is safe with me. The path you chose to walk is no one's business but your own. Godspeed."

I sprinted to my car and broke every traffic law on the books getting back to The Nest. Thirty minutes later and thoroughly out of breath I staggered into the concourse. There wasn't a game scheduled that day, but I flagged down an attendant to point me towards the office for the home team equipment manager. I was told to check the indoor batting cages nestled deep within the stadium's concrete-lined basement levels.

* * * * *

I opened the door to the batting cages just in time to see Charlie Milton step onto the mock home plate with a remote control gripped in his hand. At the other end of the long room a squat machine crouched on the mock pitcher's mound like some giant prehistoric insect, overhead lights gleaming on its black metallic shell. The equipment manager smiled at me.

"Afternoon Mr. Nelson, I wondered if I was gonna see ya again."

I held up my hands. "It's over Charlie, please don't do anything you're going to regret."

He smirked ruefully. "How'd ya figure out it was little ol' me?"

"I saw some deep gouge marks in the dirt of the pitcher's mound while examining Peterson's body. I didn't make the connection until I heard about his pitching machines this morning. I had been working on the theory that a human threw the baseball that killed Mr. Peterson."

Charlie's gut shook with deep, hearty laughter. "Every time it's always the devil inna details that trips ya up."

"Where is that baseball anyway, Charlie?"

"In m' desk sealed in a plastic bag. I stuck a writt'n confession in there wit' the thing. Three weeks ago Bud Crowley came back to The Nest to throw out the first pitch for one of the home games. Later that day I overheard him talking with Marty Graham about how Peterson had screwed 'em both over in some fancy money deal. That was the last straw for me; I had already heard rumors from the front office about Old Man Peterson plotting to move the 'Hawks out to Las Vegas."

Charlie looked up at me. Tears glistened in his eyes. "I put up with his crap for twenny years, I wasn't gonna stand for it any longer. I sent an anonymous note telling him I knew everything. I told him to be at home plate by midnight or my story was going right to them folks in the press. I set up one of the machines an' cut the juice to the stadium's lights. As soon as he set foot on home plate I hit the switch and fed his sorry ass a hundred-mile-an-hour fastball."

I met Charlie's wide-eyed stare head on. "Charlie, believe me when I say I know what it's like to lose your livelihood when you live and breathe baseball. But you can move on. I, I know you're better than this, put the remote down and let's talk about it. Please."

Charlie's grinned. "I only got one thing left to say." His grin widened maniacally. "BATTER UP!!"

He pushed the button. That damned pitching machine screamed. A white blur took the man full in the face. The remains of Charlie Milton crumpled to the ground. I closed my eyes and sighed. Another runner, cut down at the plate.

* * * * *

I made two calls in the following three minutes. First, I called Mrs. Peterson and extracted a promise from her to keep my name out of the papers. I told her the whole tale and made an appointment to return the datebook in two hours. After I hung up with her I dialed the number for Detective Portman. I told him what had happened and where I was. He sprinted through the front doors of The Nest twenty minutes later. He found the murder weapon and confession right where Charlie had left them. He promised to keep my name out of the story on the condition that I make a statement for the record back at the precinct. I agreed, and made it to Mrs. Peterson's house with five minutes to spare.

The press broke the story the next day; I made it a point to stay home and ignore the rest of the planet. Later that week I found myself in a bar two blocks from my office sipping a beer. Everyone was talking about the strike; the City Council had finally given in, and the trash collectors were back at work keeping Edge City relatively clean. I listened to a 7 o'clock news broadcast on the matter for a few minutes, then asked the barkeep to switch the channel over to sports, where the BayHawks were facing down the Phillies. During the sixth inning one of the broadcasters took a break from the play-by-play to tell a brief story. His voice rustled through the bar like fresh sandpaper.

"The Edge City BayHawks are no strangers to injury. One major reason they've struggled for so long is their star players' inability to stay healthy. Of course few examples are more heartbreaking than their star young catcher from the '94 season, where they came within three games of making the playoffs for the first time in twenty years. However, after a nasty home plate collision on the last day of the season gave him a broken arm, wrist, elbow, and shoulder, Billy Brown dropped out of sight and never played baseball again. Perhaps one day we'll find out what happened to him. Until then, we're proud to bring you BayHawks baseball here on Channel 10!"

I waited for the game to come back on. When it did, I ordered another beer and thought about tomorrow.

2012

Sliding into Darkness

Jennifer Louden

July

She arose suddenly, not sure why, and reached for her iPhone. 3:12 AM. She could tell she was alone in the bed. "Where is he?" she thought. Usually when he slept downstairs she could hear the hum of the television, but tonight was different. Carefully, so not to wake the children, she moved toward the stairs. Still no noise and downstairs was pitch black. She searched the family room. Nothing. He had been there, the rumpled blanket was on the floor and the feather pillow still bore his head imprint. But he was gone. Her face heated and tears began to form. "Where is he?" She peered out of the front window. Even in the darkness she could see that his minivan was not in the driveway. The tree-lined suburban Maryland street was dark and quiet. Everything looked so innocent. She was not as careful going back up the stairs until the oldest made a noise. She stopped quickly and waited. One more whimper and then back to sleep. She ran to her room and closed the door.

At 4:45 AM her alarm buzzed, but she was already awake sitting on the edge of the bed. She showered, brushed her teeth, did her hair, and threw on a clean pair of scrubs. She didn't cry. The kids were still asleep. Downstairs in the kitchen, she pulled together a lunch and sipped on steaming hot coffee. "Just breathe," she thought. "Just grab your bag and go." So she did. Sneakers on, bag over shoulder, car keys in her hand. She walked out of the kitchen, through the family room and out the front door.

In the car she cried. She had walked past him in the family room. He was on the couch with his back towards her under the covers. He never said a word.

August

Monica Fells was sitting nervously outside my Washington, D.C. office. She was the last appointment of the day and I was grateful for her punctuality. "Hi, I'm Nina Langston," I said. "Come on in." She shot up so quickly that her massive tote bag flew off her lap and onto the floor. As she gathered her belongings I noticed her almost white roots pushing up from her scalp. The rest of her short cropped hair was a deep chestnut. Her scrubs were wrinkled and mismatched. The hospital I.D. badge was clipped to her breast pocket and the other pockets overflowed with crumpled papers. I gave a quick nod of thanks to Shirleen, the receptionist, and closed my office door.

"Have a seat, please. Do you want some coffee?"

"Uh, no...but thanks. I'm already full of caffeine. And I'm still tired."

"What can I do for you today?"

She looked exhausted. "My husband has been going out at night."

"What do you mean?" I said.

"He's been sleeping in our family room instead of in our bedroom for a while now. About a month ago I noticed that he's been sneaking out of the house at night."

"Have you asked him about it?" Obvious question, but you would be amazed how many people come to my office without asking that question.

"No."

Just like I thought. So, he's cheating and she wants me to find out why, with whom, et cetera, et cetera. "And you would like for me to..."

"To figure out why. I mean, where is he going?" She was becoming frustrated.

"OK, let's take a step back." I pushed back my chair and moved around to the front of my desk. I couldn't tell if she was upset about her husband or if it was exhaustion, or both. "Tell me what's happening and I'll let you know if I can help."

"We've just not been connecting lately. Know what I mean? I knew that things weren't great, but we have three kids. I'm not saying that he's cheating. I just don't know and I want to find out. The first night I noticed he was gone I wanted to die, but I didn't know what to do or say." She gave me all the details.

"So this started about a month ago?"

"I think. I mean, that's when I became aware."

"How often does he do this?"

"I've been keeping track. It's usually 4 or 5 times a week. Here you go." She handed me a crumpled paper from her pocket.

"And you want me to figure out where he's going and why, right?" I tried to uncrumple the paper without tearing it. This will need to be scanned and the paper copy kept here in my files. The last thing we need is him finding this.

"Yes." She was embarrassed.

"Look, don't worry about this. Men are always running around. In my experience, they're not very smart about it. I'm sure that I can help you put this together." Her eyes were glassy, but she wasn't crying. "Are you OK at home? Do you think you are in danger? Do you think your children are in danger? I have to ask."

"Yes, I'm OK. We are all OK. Thanks."

"Well, Mrs. Fells—"

"Call me Monica."

"Monica, I think I can help you. Let's get some info and get started."

I woke up the next morning at 4:45 a.m. as usual. Bailey and Finn were up, eager to go out. They licked my face coaxing me out of bed. Bailey weighs about 125 pounds but thinks that he is a lap dog. Rottweilers are amazing. Finn, a Doberman, is leaner at 87 pounds. He's more aware of his size and definitely aware of Bailey's size. They share a bed in my room. Bailey has his own bed, but since he thinks he is a puppy, he snuggles with Finn instead. When I left the K-9 unit, I cried for three days. Not because I missed my job, but because I missed my K-9 partner, Poppy. I adopted Bailey and Finn two weeks later. While I know how sweet they are, I keep that to myself. It's better if everyone assumes they're mean. Bailey and Finn are well trained and extremely loyal to me. If I needed them to chase or catch someone, they could on command. It has only happened once. Usually just the threat of them is enough to keep people in line. If Monica Fells noticed them behind my desk yesterday, she said nothing. My guess is that she had no idea. Good boys, very good boys.

While Bailey and Finn devoured their breakfast, I changed into my running clothes. This is the part of the day I get the most thinking done. I don't listen to music while I run for safety, but also because it allows me to think. The dogs, full and satisfied, went back to bed. Typical. I grabbed my pepper spray, hat, keys, and Garmin, and was out the door. It was a typical hot and steamy D.C. August morning. I could feel sweat droplets of sweat on my back before I made the first turn off the block.

So Monica's husband has been sneaking out of the house regularly for at least a month. He says nothing, she says nothing. I feel sorry for her. They've been married for 15 years and this is how he treats her. Mile one, 8:18. Nice warm up. Time for the real work. Mile 2, 8:00. Mile 3, 7:48. Mile 4, 7:43. Mile 5, 7:38. I cooled down back to my apartment. I peeled off my clothes and hopped in the shower. I pulled a short cotton sleeveless dress over my head, ate breakfast, and was ready to go. Bailey and Finn were waiting by the door. "Ready, boys? Let's go!"

My office building on H Street has several businesses. Langston & Langston, L.L.C. is located on the third floor. My firm shares Shirleen, the receptionist, with the small tax firm next door. Sometimes they hire me for small jobs. They pay me by preparing my taxes and keeping me out of jail. I set up their security system. Symbiotic. Oh, and they also keep Bailey and Finn full of treats and belly rubs. Spoiled bastards. After forty-five minutes of internet stalking, I learned that Owen Fells was born here in D.C., went to Gonzaga and then to American University. A real D.C. native. Nothing I didn't already know. He's at work today on K Street at Abbott VanDyke Hall, a tony law firm. As a paralegal his hours are long and he makes pretty good money. According to Monica, he has lunch every Wednesday with a high school buddy. I'll be there too. Just collecting intel. I want to know what his routine is like. And maybe I'll get a few more things too.

Owen was tall and dark-skinned with a closely shaved head and a neatly trimmed goatee. Abbott VanDyke Hall is known for its bold approach to client defense. It has offices all over the world, but the headquarters are right here in D.C. Like all of the K Street firms, the employees dress conservatively in dark suits even in the summer heat. Owen is no different. He strolled out of the office at 11:50 a.m. and headed west. It must be freezing in the office because he still had his suit jacket on and didn't take it off for two blocks. Even with the jacket on, I could tell that he's well built, very muscular. Monica said he spends a lot of time in the gym. I guess you have to stay fit for the ladies. He prefers weight lifting to cardio. A plus for me, I focus on both. At 6'2 he towers over my 5'5 slim frame. In all my years no one has ever caught me in a foot chase and I've always managed to run down someone I'm chasing. Yes, they might sprint ahead, but I always catch up. I managed to blend in with the lunch crowd. He had no idea I was following him. All the while I made mental notes of his physique, gate, and mannerisms. If I lost him, or needed to pull back, I needed to be able to pick him out on a crowded street.

Owen and his friend met at Pret-A-Manger on the corner of Connecticut and K. I slipped in behind him. His friend, Steven, arrived shortly after. They grabbed a booth and immediately started talking. I was able to secure the booth behind them. It was too loud to hear their conversation. I pulled out my laptop to see if I could get into Owen's phone. Luckily he was logged into the Wi-Fi. Not smart. I easily located his phone and started reading his email. If people only knew how easy this is. His personal email was pretty boring. I downloaded as much as I could while continuing to read. My network was slowing down. Damn it. I was so engrossed in what I was doing that when his phone rang I jumped. I saved the number. It must have been work because the tone of his voice changed and he quickly gathered his things while apologizing to Steve. Shit, I need more time.

Quickly, I grabbed a pair of huge sunglasses and a baseball cap out of my bag. I threw my computer in my bag and rushed past both of them, knocking Owen ever so slightly. Outside, I continued west on K, knowing that Owen would head east. I sat on a bench in the service lane and pulled his phone out of my bag. In seconds, I had his SIM card plugged into my laptop. Come on, come on, come on. Five minutes later, I had as much as I could get without letting too much time pass. With the SIM card back in his phone, I started back towards Pret-A-Manger. He would be back soon. "This phone was in my booth." I told the first employee I saw. He didn't even have time to respond. I was already on my way out. No sunglasses, no hat. I again passed Owen. He even held the door for me. Thanks, man. I disappeared into the chaos of K Street. Three minutes later Owen walked out again, the phone plastered to his ear.

According to Owen's calendar, he'd be at work all afternoon meeting with three attorneys on a major case. That gave me time to head home and take a quick snooze. Apparently I'll be out late tonight.

"Hi, Monica? This is Nina. Sorry to call you at work. Is now a good time to talk?" I wanted to give her a quick update. I'd already spent a lot of her money.

"Yes, let me just go into the stairwell. How are you?"

"Good. I saw Owen at work and at lunch. Just like you said." I was feeling confident. My voice was high and quick. I needed to slow down. Breathe. "I also got his phone."

"You have his phone?"

"Well, *had* his phone. I made sure he got it back. After I got as much as I could from it."

"Isn't that illegal? Are you going to get in trouble? What if he finds out?"

"He's not going to find out." I didn't respond to the legal question. She didn't ask again. Look, it's mid-afternoon and I'd only done one...OK, two semi-illegal things. It wasn't my fault he used the Wi-Fi. I rang off and drove back to the office. Shirleen gave me a huge smile.

"How are the pups?"

"They're fine. I don't know how you get them to do that. Not one peep. Maybe one day you can teach me so I can get my mutt to behave?" She always wanted to know my secrets. Shirleen has worked for us for about six months. Her background check was fine, but I take time to open up to folks. When your business is other people's business you learn to keep a low profile.

"Yes, Shirleen, as soon as I have some free time." I closed the door behind me. Bailey and Finn greeted me with lots of tail wags and grunts. Then it was back to sleep. Tough life. I got to work on Owen's phone. What have you been up to, Mr. Fells? I scrolled through his email. Nothing very interesting. Then I moved on to his text messages. More interesting. Lots and lots of messages. This was going to take a while.

About 30 minutes later there was a soft and familiar knock at my door. One knock, followed by two quick knocks, followed by one knock. "Come on in, Mom!" She poked her head in first. The pups, who were in deep sleep, quickly rose and greeted her. She and my father were the original Langston & Langston. "Ah, my grandbabies! The only grands I will ever know."

"Mom, really?" We went through this all the time. My mother, Jacqueline, is sixty-eight but she looks no more than fifty. We are both athletic with runner bodies. Small frames but extremely powerful. I started running with my mom when I was five. She has been a runner her entire life. Three years ago I ran my first ultra marathon. A tough 50 mile race out in Loudoun County Virginia. It was her 17th 50 miler. She beat me by forty-five seconds. In November we'll run the JFK 50. I really want to beat her.

My father, Benjamin, passed away three years ago from leukemia. He served on the DC police force as a detective for 27 years before he retired and opened a private investigation firm, Langston & Langston. My mother was a housewife, but her life was never typical. She was my father's trusted confidante. Together they worked all of his cases. I would listen from upstairs while they talked and laughed late into the night. I knew I wanted to be just like them. For ten years they ran the agency together. I left the force exactly one month after my father died. He always wanted me to work at the agency and it was finally time. I learned everything from my parents. I hoped my father would be proud.

"I thought you would be at home? You're retired, you should be enjoying your life outside of this office."

"Just checking in to see what's happening with this new case."

"I didn't tell you about the new case." Clearly she has been speaking to Shirleen.

"A little birdie told me. Is there anything I can do?"

"As I'm sure you already know, the client's husband is stepping out at night. She wants me to figure out where he's going and why. You wanna read some text messages?"

"Cheating husbands are my favorite! Give me those messages."

"I'm thinking cheating too. But let's try to keep it open for now. It won't take long to confirm. If he is cheating, he has left a trail. Cheaters always think they are being sneaky."

We spent the next hour going through all of Owen's texts I was able to download. Mom never asked how I obtained this information. He had several contacts with initials only. Those messages appeared to be in code. Letters and numbers, no symbols. Hmm. I looked at mom and she knew what I was thinking. I picked up my office phone and dialed.

"6569." The voice was firm and direct.

"Hey, it's me. I need to talk to you. Do you have time today?"

"Not today. Tomorrow for lunch?"

"Yeah, that will work. I'll meet you at our usual spot."

"Our *favorite*—"

"Good-bye."

Mom said nothing, but I could see one eyebrow raised while she continued to read through the text messages. It was 4:00. I needed to get home, hopefully rest a bit, and change before going out again. "Would you mind taking the dogs? I'm going to work tonight. Hopefully Mr. Fells will go out."

"Yes, darling. Of course." Instinctively, Bailey and Finn rose, stretched and went to the door. I walked to the door with mom. She really does love her grandbabies.

"Thanks, mom. I'll pick them up tomorrow morning."

"Be careful tonight."

"Always. Bye, boys. Be good." After they were gone I checked my email and finished a final report for my last case. By 6:30 I was heading home.

I crawled into bed. Monica said she goes to bed around 10. Owen won't be going anywhere before that. I set my phone for 8:00 and drifted into sleep. I jumped out of bed at the sound of the alarm. After a quick shower and a fresh change of clothes I ate a tuna sandwich and caught the local news on Channel 8. Homicide, theft, another Metro meltdown. Ah, typical D.C. day.

My preparation for surveillance was always specific and precise. I made sure to have a picture of the person on my phone and if possible a picture of the vehicle. I'd already memorized his license plate. I filled the tank with gas on the way home. You never know how far you might have to drive. My 2011 Honda CR-V blended in everywhere. My surveillance bag was always packed and ready to go. It contained my DSLR camera and extra zoom lens, two bottles of SMART water, one pack of mint gum, a non-descript baseball cap, a Taser that looks like brass knuckles, and a retractable baton. I didn't carry a gun. Too many things could go wrong. I'd rather run or beat someone's ass with my baton. If someone gets his hands on me, I'd use the Taser. I didn't expect trouble tonight. I just wanted to observe.

I arrived in Northern Silver Spring at 9:45 pm and waited down the street from the Fells residence. Monica sent me a text at 10:00 saying she'll "check the chart tomorrow," our code for heading to bed. Both cars were parked in the driveway. I turned my car around and parked on the opposite side of the street. Around 11:30, the front door opened. Owen wore all black and appeared to be carrying an empty duffel bag. He backed out of the driveway with the lights off and drove past me. He turned his lights on at the end of the block. I followed. We headed south on Georgia Avenue. Twenty minutes later we crossed into D.C. He wasn't driving fast and traffic was light this time of night. At Florida Ave. he made a hard left. I ran the red to keep up. Another left onto New York Ave. and we were heading back in the direction of Maryland. He was careful to obey the speed limit, obviously aware of the speed cameras every 100 yards. He slowed at Missouri and turned into the Comfort Inn. Interesting.

The District, like many cities, has struggled to manage the homeless population. Most at risk are mothers with small children. The shelters are filled to capacity. In response, D.C. started using a couple of motels along New York Avenue as a shelter for homeless women. Owen parked his car at the Comfort Inn and walked to the Checkers with the duffel bag. A few minutes later he came out with two bags and two drinks. He walked into the front entrance of the motel and disappeared from sight. He appeared on the second floor of the motel's exterior corridors moments later. I took several photos with the zoom lens. He knocked on the door of room 218, the door opened but I could not see who opened it. I think I saw a smile on his face as he entered the room. I grabbed my phone and dialed the Comfort Inn's number. "Comfort Inn, how may I help you?"

"Room 218." I half whispered.

"One moment."

The phone rang four times before she picked up. "Hello?"

The voice was tentative and high pitched. She sounded young.

"Sandra?"

"Ain't nobody here by that name."

"Well, where the hell is she?"

"I *said* you have the wrong number." Click.

I thought about calling back, but didn't want to risk it. I'll find her tomorrow. At 3:15 am Owen left the room. This time the duffel bag looked full. Snap, snap, snap. I tried to get a picture of her, but she stayed out of view. Back in his car, Owen pulled out of the lot and headed back the way we came. I made sure he went home and then headed back into N.E. After I arrived home, I made some notes and recorded my thoughts. Then it was time for sleep.

At 7:42 am Monica was blowing up my cell phone. "Well? Where did he go? I know he went out. I couldn't sleep and heard him leave."

I sat up in bed and rubbed my eyes. "Good morning to you too, Monica."

"Sorry, I just want to know what happened. I don't have a lot of time."

"He went to a motel on New York Avenue –"

"That bastard."

"I don't know who he saw. I'll find out today. Monica, it's very important that you don't do anything stupid. I'm keeping you informed, but if you go off, I won't tell you anything else. Understand? Try to be calm."

"Yes. Calm."

"You cannot let him know you're suspicious. I don't want him to change his routine."

"Yes. Calm. I have to go."

"We'll talk soon." She didn't say goodbye. I called Mom and told her I'd be over in 45 minutes. She was out of breath, just back from her run. Damn it. She's going to beat me at JFK. Freshly showered and blood pumping caffeine, I made my way to the office. The pups sat in the back seat with their faces pressed to the glass. Reluctantly, I cracked the window. It was already 85 degrees. They clamored over each other to sniff the air.

"Well, you look tired today." Shirleen always knows how to brighten my day.

"Thanks, Shirleen." I closed my office door behind me and sat at my desk. Bailey and Finn went right to sleep. While the computer booted up, I checked my email on my phone and scrolled through Facebook. More and more friends with husbands and babies. I closed the app and got on the computer. A quick Google search gave me all the info I needed on the Comfort Inn. In the closet I found a pair of cut-off jeans and a white tank top. I put some gel in my short natural and rummaged through my desk for my gold hoop earrings. "I'll be back after lunch, could you take the pups out for me? Text me if you need anything."

"Your outfit is interesting. Don't worry about the dogs, I'll make sure they go out."

I made my way to the Comfort Inn and parked with a perfect view of Room 218. According to the *Washington Post* expose, the women here tend to gather at the pool while the kids are at school. Given today's heat, I wasn't sure that anyone would be out, but sure enough the women slowly filtered out of their rooms and down to the pool. I was anxious, where was "not Sandra" in room 218? Eventually the door opened and "not Sandra" emerged. She couldn't have been more than 16 or 17. And she was carrying a baby. This is not good. I waited for her to make it to the pool before I got out of the car. I didn't go through the front entrance. Instead, I went around the side and slipped in through the pool entrance. Not exactly secure. I walked around the perimeter and posted up three chairs away from "not Sandra" and her baby. She was too busy talking on the phone to even notice me.

"Yeah, he's an asshole. I need to stop messing around with him...I know, I know." She smacked her gum and bounced the little baby boy.

"He was here last night...Of course not." The baby was starting to fuss. "I gotta go, he's acting up."

Behind my pitch black sunglasses I pretended to text while I took several pictures of "not Sandra" and her baby boy. Another woman approached her and they chatted for a bit. It was so hot. Baby boy settled into his mother's arms and closed his eyes. I rose and walked in their direction. "Do you know where to get breakfast around here?"

"There's a Checkers right over there, or you can go to McDonald's a little further down." She pointed down New York Avenue.

"Thanks, your baby is so cute. How old is he?"

"He's ten months and growing like crazy. His name's Jerrod."

"I'm Nina." I said as I gingerly approached. "It's so damn hot out here."

"Who you telling? I'm Tiffany." She held out her left hand, Jerrod was sleeping in her right arm. I gently shook her hand with my left.

"Nice to meet you."

"I haven't seen you here." She looked directly at me, but not in a suspicious way.

"I'm new, hopefully won't be here long. I can't believe I'm even here."

"Yeah, but it's better than the shelter. At least you get your own room and the door locks."

"I'm going over to McDonald's. You want something?"

"No, I'm good. We ate earlier and I have water and some snacks in my bag."

"OK, I'll be back." I left the pool area through the unsecure fence and made my way down the street. Tiffany and Jerrod were both so young. Was Owen really seeing this girl? If she's as young as I thought she was, he is doing more than having an affair. He's committing statutory rape. Was Jerrod his? I didn't want to freak her out by asking too many questions. I wasn't going to tell Monica about this until I knew more. I made my way back to the pool with an iced coffee and an Egg McMuffin, the least offensive thing on the menu. I grabbed a bottle of water out of my car making sure Tiffany did not see me.

"You been on the streets long?" She asked as soon as I sat down.

"On and off for as long as I can remember. Basically when I don't have a boyfriend." I winked at her and sipped my iced coffee.

"I get it. I'm just trying to get on my feet. My boyfriend can't afford to have us with him now." My ears perked up, but I remained silent. She said no more of the boyfriend.

We continued talking, but she didn't reveal anything else of interest. I excused myself thirty minutes later. The heat was oppressive, even under the tree. Tiffany got up from her chair at the same time. "You headed inside?" She asked.

"Yeah, I'm done with this heat. Need to make a phone call first. Nice meeting you." I scurried off into the motel. Tiffany made her way to the second floor and into her room. I avoided the front desk clerk and ducked into the bathroom to freshen up. I had a lunch date.

Back in my air conditioned CR-V, I cruised up the BW Parkway. He texted me twice while I was at the pool. We were meeting at Grillfire in Hanover near his office. I had Owen's text coded text messages. I waited in the parking lot for him to arrive. When I looked in the vanity mirror my hair was a mess. I did the best I could with it and put on some lip gloss. He arrived and parked next to me. I could see the smirk on his face when I hopped out of the car.

"Nice outfit."

"Shut it, I'm working."

Inside we sat in our usual booth. I immediately pulled out my phone and showed him Owen's texts. Josh and I met in graduate school. My undergraduate degree in computer engineering wasn't that useful while I was a detective, but really came in handy when I started working at the agency. To supplement what I already knew about hardware, I decided to pursue my Master's in cyber security. Josh spent 10 years in the Air Force. He used the G.I. post 9/11 bill to pay for graduate school. We sat next to each other the first night of our first class. After his honorable discharge, Josh went where many Air Force men and women go, the National Security Agency. He is brilliant. Most people assume that Air Force folks fly planes and that's it. Not so. Josh has never flown a plane. He has a knack for mathematics. He's a code maker and breaker. The first time I saw him outside of class we met at the National Cryptologic Museum. It is the only public interaction regular U.S. citizens can have with the NSA. He's helped me several times. We never discuss this over the phone or via text. Only in person. All phone calls to and from the NSA are monitored and so is his cell phone. No one answers the phone with a name, just a four-digit number. The main NSA building sits on the west side of the Baltimore-Washington Parkway. It is connected both above and underground to Ft. Meade which sits on the east side of the Parkway. Should the U.S. be attacked, the safest places to be are the White House and the NSA.

"Take a look at these messages. What do you think?"

"So, we're getting right to it. No small talk today? You're not even going to tell me why you are in that outfit?"

"You know how we don't talk about your job?"

"Yeah, but my job is—"

"So is mine." I pushed my cell phone in his face and looked at the menu.

"This won't take me long." He took notes on a pad he pulled from inside his back pocket. So old school. When did it become safer to write things down rather than keeping them electronically? We both ordered turkey club sandwiches. I guzzled three glasses of water. He watched me but said nothing. I could tell that even though he was staring at me he was already working on the code in his head. "I need to get back."

"How are the pups?" Only those close to me call them pups. Everyone else says dogs.

"They're great." I let down my guard a little. "This morning they were both so cute trying to hang their heads out of the window. I wanted to—"

I put my guard back up. He almost got me. "I can call you tomorrow?"

"Of course."

I threw down a twenty, grabbed my bag and phone, and headed to my car. I heard him say, "Good to see you." But I didn't turn around.

Back on the Parkway I put on a podcast and tried to get Josh off my mind. Being around him is complicated. I arrived back at the office in the early afternoon and wrote up my notes. I needed to find out Tiffany's last name. I thought about all the different ways I could go about it. I could call the hotel and see if I could get it out of the desk clerk. I could try to get it out of her tomorrow. Or, I could lift her wallet and check her I.D. Of course I decided on the slightly illegal one. I'm not going to steal her money. She won't even know it's gone. And I'll be sure she gets it back.

Between the heat and lack of sleep, I needed to get home and regroup. I said an early goodbye to Shirleen and headed home with the pups. Instead of showering right away, I decided to nap. The thought of sleep was more powerful than my stench. When I opened my eyes, the sun was settled in the west. I checked my phone. Several text messages and five missed calls. I scrolled through, nothing urgent. Well, Monica called. She thinks it's urgent. I'll get back to her later. Finn raised his head and grunted. Someone was at the front door. The knock followed. As trained, Bailey and Finn barked until I gave them the signal that all is OK. I could see Josh's face through the peephole.

"I know you're there. I heard the pups bark and then go silent. Open up."

"Hold on." I yelled. I took a deep breath and opened the door. He had changed his clothes and was now wearing khaki shorts and a U.S.A.F. t-shirt. He smelled so good. And then I remembered what I had on and that I never bothered to shower. Shit.

"Is this outfit a thing now?"

"What are you doing here?"

"Do you really want to have this discussion on your front porch?"

I rolled my eyes and let him in. Bailey and Finn were ecstatic. I haven't seen their tails wag so hard in a long time. I gave them a nod and they both ran to Josh. Traitors.

"I really wish we could have pups."

"Too bad your wife is allergic. And your daughters." That came out sharper than I wanted. "Won't they start sneezing the minute you get home?"

"They're in New York with Sharon's parents." He walked into the kitchen and opened the fridge. He took out a beer and sat on the couch.

"Well, that explains why you are here. Did you figure out those messages?"

"Jesus, can't we have a normal conversation?"

I sighed deeply.

"Yes, I figured it out. It's pretty simplistic. How about we go and get something to eat and I tell you about it?" He looked hopeful.

I looked at the clock. 7:30 pm. I had time before I needed to be up in Silver Spring.

"Umm, OK."

"You are going to shower, right?" I hurled a decorative throw pillow across the room and hit him square in the face. Years of target practice.

"Yes, jerk."

After that "first date" at the Cryptologic Museum we were inseparable. I knew he was married and had two little girls. But we were just friends and had a lot in common. Plus, he seemed miserable in his marriage. We laughed all the time. I knew all of his secrets and he knew mine. Typically we would hang out after class. It all seemed so innocent. The first time he kissed me I melted. Everything spiraled after that. Suddenly we were going back to my house after class instead of going out to eat. He would stay later and later. I fell hard. I didn't even think about his wife and kids. They were unreal to me. He barely discussed them and I chose not to ask many questions. When my father died and I left the force, he was the one who comforted me and wiped the tears from my eyes. He stayed with me for an entire week. I never asked what he told his wife or what he told his job. I simply enjoyed our time. He supported my decision to take over our family business and let my mother retire. He was more confident in my ability than I ever was. Mom knew I was seeing someone, the lack of details tipped her off that something was not right about it. Although she never said a word, I knew she figured out who he was and that he had a family. To this day we've never discussed it. Three months ago I ended it abruptly. My guilt caught up with me. And to be honest, I wanted more from him than he could ever give me. It would be easier if I never had to see him, but his assistance is invaluable. He sees things I miss and is always willing to help. Yesterday was the first time we had spoken to one another in about three weeks.

After I showered, we walked in silence down the street to Pete's Pub. Two meals together in one day.

"I've missed this place." He said after we sat down.

"Me too." I let that slip. I haven't been able to come back here since we broke up. We ordered spinach dip and a bottle of wine.

"I'm sure you're anxious to know what those messages mean."

"Most definitely."

"Are you still not carrying a gun?"

"Wha- What?"

"The messages are about drugs."

I leaned in. "Tell me everything."

"The messages are drop off and pick up locations. The different sequences refer to cocaine and heroin. Whose messages are these?"

"I'm not at liberty to say."

"You need to be careful."

"I'm always careful." Monica needs to be careful.

"Here is the key to the code. These letters are cocaine, these are heroin. It looks like four different drop off locations and one pick up location."

I looked at the key and back at the messages. "Are there times? Dates?"

"Yes. See these here? Instead of numbers, they use letters. It's not that sophisticated. I imagine a lot of people have to be able to read and understand it."

"According to this text from yesterday, there will be a pick up tonight." My mind was spinning. "I need to go."

"We didn't even eat! You can't leave yet. You need to call the police and let them sort this out. Call your old partner, he'll know what to do."

"Josh, I know what to do. I'm a detective."

"You were a detective." Low blow.

"I really appreciate you helping me with this. I can stay for the spinach dip, then I need to get going."

We made our way back to my place. I could tell that he wanted to come in, but I didn't give him the option. I thanked him again and ran up the stairs, pretending not to hear him say that he misses me.

I sat outside the Fells residence. I knew that Owen would be leaving soon. He had a job tonight. At 10:00 Monica texted me about the medical charts again. Not even five minutes later, Owen opened the front door. Early tonight. I quickly texted Monica and asked her to come outside. Owen drove past me and made a left on Georgia Avenue. I'd catch up with him later. Monica approached my car from behind. I opened the door and got out to greet her.

"What's happening? Why aren't you following him? She sounded desperate.

"I know where he's going."

"Did you find the woman?"

"Yes. Does the name Tiffany mean anything to you?"

"No. Is that her name?"

"Maybe. Listen Monica, I'm still not sure what is really going on. Tonight will be helpful. Do you have a spare key for Owen's car?"

"Yes, I'll go and get it."

It might not have been the best idea to tell her about Tiffany, but I wanted to see if any recognition showed on her face. Clients lie all the time. They leave out important facts and gloss over anything that might make them look bad. Monica seemed genuine. I needed to confirm the drug running and then let Monica know. She and her kids are not safe if Owen is wrapped up in drugs and underage girls.

"Here you go. Thanks for all that you're doing."

"It's not out of the goodness of my heart." I said jokingly. A tiny smile escaped her lips. I hopped back in the car and headed south.

I crossed the Anacostia River and found the warehouse easily. I drove by once and observed the parked cars. Owen's minivan wasn't there. The street was active, but I decided to wait in the car. Soon after, Owen's minivan pulled around the corner and parked in front of the building. I took several pictures of him carrying that duffel bag inside. Then the passenger side door opened and she emerged. Tiffany looked around anxiously and quickly ran into the warehouse. Where is Jerrod? Is he in the van? My curiosity won out and despite the possibility of getting caught, I darted across the street to check out the minivan.

I looked in all of the windows. Thankfully no Jerrod. He must be at the hotel with a friend. I hope he's not alone. I used the spare key to open the rear driver's side door. Blasted electronic doors take forever. I did a quick look around the interior. Nothing. The warehouse door opened and two men came out with duffel bags. My breath caught in my throat. I pressed the key fob and let the door close. The warehouse door opened again and there they were. The door was clicking shut. I ducked and scooted behind the van. They were arguing and distracted on the passenger's side. Tiffany's large fake Louis Vuitton sat open on the curb while she and Owen went back and forth. They moved to the front of the vehicle and continued around to the driver's side, apparently arguing about who would drive. I pulled my hat down over my eyes and walked with purpose on the passenger's side. With a quick swoop down, I had her wallet. Even though I desperately wanted to hear what they were saying, I kept moving and circled the block. They were still arguing when I came around from the back, crossed the street and got in my car. I pulled out Tiffany's I.D. and part of the puzzle came together. Tiffany Fells, age 17. Fells. I knew there was something familiar about Tiffany. It's the eyes. She and Owen have the same eyes. Tiffany is not his side piece, she's his daughter. But why are they running drugs together? The minivan whisked by me. I threw Tiffany's wallet in the passenger's seat and threw the car into gear. I didn't want to lose them.

For the next few hours father and daughter delivered drugs all over the city. At 2:00 am they returned to the warehouse with a duffel bag full of cash. Again, Tiffany waited in the car while Owen went inside. It's now or never. I grabbed my baton and slid it down the back of my pants.

I tapped gently on the window, trying not to startle Tiffany. I failed. She nearly jumped out of her skin. She could not place me at first, but the recognition slowly came to her face. Her eyes darted from side to side.

"Nina? What are you doing here?"

"Sorry I scared you. Can we talk?" I sensed a presence behind me. Tiffany's eyes moved ever so slightly off my gaze. I pivoted and grabbed my baton from the back of my pants. With a swift knee to the groin, Owen was on the ground. He tried to get up, but he could not move. I purposefully did not use all of the force I could have. The man might want to have more children. "Get up, Owen. Get in your car and drive back to the Comfort Inn. I'll follow behind." I reached down to help him off the ground. "Let's go. Your wife is worried." His face fell.

Back at the hotel, Owen and I sat across from each other in Tiffany's room while she went to pick up Jerrod from her friend down the hall.

"Who are you and how do you know who I am?"

"My name is Nina Langston. I'm a private investigator. Your wife hired me after she noticed you sneaking out of the house at night. She assumed you were seeing another woman. She was right."

"Tiffany is my daughter! I'm no pedophile!"

"I know she is your daughter." I handed back Tiffany's wallet. "Why are you doing this? Running around for drug dealers? Keeping your daughter a secret from your wife? And your grandson?"

He looked down at his hands and said nothing. I figured that Tiffany must be in trouble with some dealer. Owen was trying to help her, but really he was digging himself into a hole. "Owen?"

"Tiffany reached out to me last month. I didn't even know she existed. I fooled around a bit when Monica and I were dating. But as soon as we got engaged, I stopped. Tiffany's mother never told me anything."

"Where's her mother now?"

"I don't know. Strung out somewhere. Tiffany was smoking weed. Nothing serious, but when her mom got really bad, she started sampling from her stash. Tiffany got messed up on heroin, smoking and snorting it. She hates needles. When she got pregnant, she went into a treatment center to get clean for the baby."

"I'm glad she could get clean. How did she end up running drugs?"

"Her mother was dealing for Big Sugar, at the warehouse. But, of course, she shot up more than she sold and he wants his money. When she disappeared, he came for Tiffany. She started working for him out of fear. After a couple of months, she called me and we met. I'm just trying to help her."

"But you are risking everything. Your marriage, your family, your job!"

"She's my daughter and I was never there for her." Tiffany arrived back with Jerrod sound asleep in her arms. She placed him in the center of the bed and surrounded him with pillows.

"You need to tell Monica about this. And you need to get out of this business. I have police contacts, they can help you."

Owen shook his head. "We can't. Big Sugar will find Tiffany."

"I'm going to call Monica in the morning. She will know either way. She knows how to reach me if you want help." I rose from my chair and took one last look at Jerrod. His chest fluttered with quick baby breaths.

I pulled onto my block, not even sure what time it was. I could see him sitting on my porch when I parked the car. I climbed out, sighed heavily and walked up the stairs. The key slid easily in the front door and I went inside. Josh followed behind me and shut the door.

September

My morning runs are much cooler now that summer has broken. All of the hot and humid training has paid off. Perhaps I can beat Mom at JFK?

Owen and Monica are no longer in Maryland. At least I don't think they are. Tiffany and Jarrod are gone too. A few nights after I last spoke to Monica and told her everything, the police conducted a raid at the warehouse. A friend in the department couldn't confirm or deny that Owen had anything to do with that. If there's a trial, my guess is that they'll suddenly reappear. I wish them luck, they're going to need it.

Josh stayed with me for two days and nights. It was glorious and terrible at the same time. As soon as his wife and kids were back, he left. The pups were visibly distraught when he packed his bag. I couldn't even speak. I haven't called him, he hasn't called me. We're both better off.

2016

It Needed Doing

Carl Kinkel

I t was nighttime, and I was standing there in the pouring rain, waiting for the police to arrive. I felt devoid of all emotion. I just stood there in the rain, smoke curling from the barrel of my gun, and waited. I was waiting for something, the sound of a siren, the telltale red and blue flash of an approaching police car, and the nervous shouted commands of: 'Freeze! GUN! Drop it!' Hillsborough County Sherriff deputies were not known for being either gentle or patient. It wouldn't matter that I was a licensed PI, that my cause was just, or that the man I had killed deserved what he got. At that moment, all the cops would have seen is a potential nut job standing over a dead body. They wouldn't care why I did it. Police policy, and it was an understandable one given the world we lived in, would be to act first and ask questions later. So there was a really good chance I was going to get killed if I failed to comply with their commands. But none of that had happened. Not yet. So I just stood there and waited.

In retrospect, it took a lot less effort to kill him than I thought it would. All the righteous rage I once felt towards this bastard disappeared the moment I pulled the trigger. The remorse I expected to feel after killing this guy never appeared. Instead, I just felt tired. I had killed before during the war. But that was different. That was necessity, politics. It was hard not to feel remorse for killing someone who had never done you wrong before, someone you didn't know, another soldier. But killing this guy was different, this was personal. Emotionally, I was as empty as the spent shell casings lying in the pool of rapidly expanding blood that surrounded his body. I knew that if someone didn't act soon, the blood would quickly congeal on the brass casings, obliterating any fingerprints I might have left behind when I loaded my gun's magazine. I also didn't care if the cops did find my fingerprints. After all, I wasn't the one with something to hide.

At that moment I could have turned and walked away. With no witnesses, and no real clues about what had happened, there was very little to point the cops in my direction. Disappearing would have been the easiest thing in the world to do. But it wouldn't be the right thing to do. I knew that. You knew it too. At that moment, I could have driven home to our empty house, dropped face down onto our bed and slept for the first time since this nightmare, our nightmare, had begun nearly forty-eight hours ago. I could have walked away a free man. All I had to do was turn around and start slowly walking away, just disappear, my image quickly disappearing into the darkness, the rain and wind erasing any trace of my having been at the scene. No babe, I couldn't walk away from this even if I wanted to. I owed you more than that, you might not like it, but it was what I believe you deserved. You know me babe, I'm a man of my word, and when I set out to do something, I do it. Running away from a crisis wasn't my style. Running away is what he did the night he took you away from me. The drunken dog! What kind of man could do what he did? A coward, that's who; and you know how much I hate cowards.

I had chosen my kill zone carefully, executing my plan when I was sure no one would be around, especially any families. Too many families had suffered already. I wasn't about to see another one destroyed. I used the unregistered .22 caliber pistol that I kept secured in an old ammo can out in the garage. Most people imagine PI's prefer to carry .45 caliber M1911A1 automatics strapped to their armpit like some 1940's gangster. That may be true for some private dicks, but I'm not one of them. I don't even like guns that much. I'm kind of guy who prefers to solve cases using his head, like a modern day Sherlock Holmes, rather than relying on raw strength and the threat of violence. I'm no Mike Hammer wannabe…at least I wasn't until now. Besides, only idiots with giant egos and a need for attention like to walk around packing that kind of artillery. No, my little .22 caliber pocket pistol would work just fine for what I had in mind. Its small size made it easy to conceal in my pocket, where it would remain undetected until I was ready to use it.

I still remember the night the cops showed up at our door. There were two of them, a newbie and his older partner. The older cop just stood in the background stone silent and looking preoccupied. He had made too many calls just like this one in the past. I could see it in his eyes. I had seen that same look in the eyes of my fellow soldiers during the war, the look of someone who would rather be anywhere but here telling some complete stranger that a loved one was dead and would never come home. I'd delivered the same news myself when I was in the Army. It was never easy and I hated doing it. It didn't matter where it happened or how because the outcome was always the same: pain, sorrow, anguish, anger, regret, emptiness, and repeat. The same emotions would keep repeating until the mind and heart were able to come to terms with a new reality. Some people never make that adjustment, and I honestly didn't want to try to. This is probably why the old cop decided to let his younger partner deliver the news.

"I'm sorry to disturb you so late at night Sir. Sir, is your name Michael Hightower? Sir, I am afraid we have some bad news, perhaps we could go inside and sit down and talk? No? Okay. Sir, I am sorry to have to tell you this but...killed while walking...I am sorry...I don't think....Do you have someone you could call...can you come to the hospital tomorrow...again, I am sorry for your loss...I know this is hard...I'm sorry, that is all I can tell you at the moment."

I don't know what I said in response to his questions, at least not beyond asking how, when, where, and who did it. But then the older cop said, "All we know is that she was killed by a suspected drunk driver driving a red 2015 Chevy Camaro."

The younger cop looked surprised and a little caught off guard when his partner said this, but I chalked that up to nerves, both his and mine. "Do you have any kids, Mr. Hightower," the older cop asked?

"Kids, no, we don't have any kids, why?"

"No reason. I'm sorry... I'm sorry for your loss."

"Did you get the bastard that hit her?"

"No. He got away. But we will get him eventually; just leave this to us Mr. Hightower."

The old cop had run out of things to say. So we just stood there staring at each other under the harsh glow of our porch light, waiting for someone to say something, anything, before the silence suffocated us all. The silence seemed to stretch on forever, until the older cop abruptly turned on his heel and began walking back to his patrol car. Caught off guard by his partner's sudden departure, the young cop did a quick double take before issuing me one more "I am sorry for your loss Sir," before turning to catch up to his partner. They just left me standing there in the doorway, cold and angry, my world lying in tatters all around me.

The next day I went to the morgue and identified your body before filling out some mandatory paperwork authorizing them to harvest your organs, arranged for the funeral home to pick your body up, cremate you, and have your ashes interred at St. Jude's Cemetery. I stopped at the scene of the "accident" on the way home and saw where you had died. There was nothing there but a brown stain and the faint chalk outline marking where your body had come to rest on the sidewalk; some tire marks in the grass to mark your killer's passing, and not much else. While I was there I did a quick scan around the area to see if there were any traffic cameras, anything that might give me a lead on what happened and who was involved. There was a traffic light a few hundred meters down the road with a camera on it, which the police probably used to identify the car that hit you. I knew the cops weren't going to let me see the footage, at least not willingly. So I started looking for the piece of shit that took you away from me.

The sidewalk where you were killed is located in a residential neighborhood, and some of the houses were occupied. Perhaps one of the owners could tell me more. It was pure luck that the third door I knocked on would be owned by a little grey haired retiree who was more than willing to tell me everything she knew about last night's events. Better yet, she had installed a surveillance camera facing the street, overlooking her driveway, and a section of sidewalk about twenty feet away from where you'd been hit. The camera was linked to her home alarm system, allowing her to monitor anyone who came to her front door while she was away. She said she installed it to catch anyone trying to break into her house or steal her mail. The camera didn't record an image of you being hit, but it did record the image of what appeared to be a Black 1997 Jeep Wrangler swerving off the sidewalk, narrowly missing the backend of the old lady's Lincoln and her trash cans before coming to a complete stop in the middle of the road with its motor still running. A skinny drunk climbed out of the driver's seat and staggered back down the street to where your body must have been lying. Shortly after, the video caught the same individual sprinting for the jeep and speeding off down the street. To be honest, the kid didn't look evil. But then again, the devil never looks like you expect him to, and the highway to hell is often paved with good intentions. Some of the scariest monsters I had ever encountered looked like perfectly normal people. That is what made them so terrifying.

So the old cop had lied to me. I don't think the old cop knew I was a PI, but he might have, in which case his deception could be chalked up to his desire to keep me from doing exactly what I was trying to do, seek revenge. To be honest, I didn't spend too much time worrying about it. I had a score to settle.

The next day, I began reaching out to my numerous contacts in local law enforcement and government. My first call was to a gal I knew at the Florida Department of Motor Vehicles who owed me a couple of favors after I had helped find her runaway daughter. She was a good gal, just trying to make do with what she had, doing her best to make ends meet on a crap government salary. She couldn't afford to pay my full wage, so I offered her a discount in exchange for the occasional favor. It didn't take long to get a list of Black Jeep Wrangler owners. Granted, Black Jeep Wranglers were more common than dogs in Southern Florida, but it was a start. PIs don't have a lot of friends, but they do end up collecting a lot of information on people, information that can be used to get better information when the time comes. Which is why when the time came, I had no compunction whatsoever about using everything I knew about a certain Sherriff's Deputy in order to find out who owned the Black Jeep that had killed you.

I was never one to go in for blackmail. Some detectives do, but I don't. I figured people have the right to be weird in the privacy their own homes. As long as what they do for kicks isn't immoral or illegal. And in this case the 'what' happened to involve a rotund police officer with a penchant for wearing a man-sized diaper, and sucking on a huge baby bottle while a hooker named Wendy, who specialized in 'babysitting,' plied him with all kinds of 'motherly attention.' It never ceased to amaze me, though, why anyone would think recording these exploits using a digital camera hooked to an unprotected Wi-Fi network would be a good idea.

I discovered this information during the course of my investigation into his wife, who he suspected was cheating on him with another man. She was cheating on him, just not with a man, and I was able to prove it. But in the process, I had also discovered something about my client and in the end, I didn't think it was okay for him to explore his sexuality if his wife couldn't do the same thing. Which is why when it came time for them to get a divorce I decided to keep my mouth shut and bided my time. I had decided that I would deal with any guilt I felt about deceiving my client later. But I never felt guilt about doing it. Needless to say, Officer Poopy-Pants was less than pleased when I told him what I wanted, and what I was willing to do to get it. But he quickly saw reason and eight hours later I had an exact copy of the entire investigation sitting next to me on the passenger seat of my car as I drove up Interstate 4 towards Hopkinsville and the last known address of your killer.

With any luck I would soon be face to face with my wife's killer. You'd think I'd feel satisfied knowing this, but I wasn't. I wasn't satisfied because something just didn't seem right. Not the killing part. I was okay with killing this douche bag. What bugged me was the fact that the police seemed to know everything about him, but for some reason they hadn't arrested him yet. Why was that? Hell, they knew his family history, criminal record, address, everything. So why hadn't they busted him? Was he some kind of confidential informant? Or was he connected to something larger? In the end I decided I simply didn't care. I wasn't trying to solve a criminal conspiracy; I was just wanted to avenge my wife's death. But the questions kept coming, and I knew they weren't going to stop until I was completely satisfied I had the right guy. What was I missing? Did someone else kill you? I needed to know before I could act.

I stopped at a local diner and read through the case file one more time just to make sure I knew who I was chasing and where the connections lay. The diner was just like any other fast food joint I'd ever been in, with its greasy air, off-white walls, shiny black mica tabletops, and squeaky linoleum floors. It was the kind of place where the appearance of a stranger wouldn't be considered unusual and the waitresses addressed you as 'hon,' or 'honey.'

Upon entering the diner, I took a quiet booth in the back of the joint, ordered a coffee and a sandwich, and began going through the file from cover to cover. The waitress who brought me my order looked like she was going to strike up a conversation. I didn't want that so I gave her a look that clearly indicated I wanted to be left alone. Not many people can deliver this look, but I can. It was a look that said fuck off. I don't care what you say, or think, or want. Just leave me the hell alone and everything will be fine. Nine times out of ten it works very well. It works really well when you are angry, and I was plenty angry. Not at the waitress, she was just doing her job, being friendly and trying to earn herself a good tip. No, right at that moment I was angry with God, the world, the cops, and I was really angry with the guy that killed you. I channeled all of my pain and anger into that one look, and the waitress wilted away like a delicate flower that had been left out in direct sunlight for too long.

Satisfied I wasn't going to be interrupted, I re-opened the file and started to read again. The file was marked Law Enforcement Confidential, and as far as police records go it was pretty good. Inside I found the life history – what there was of it – of one Lonny M Spate, 21 years old. Caucasian, standing 5'10" tall and weighing 168 lbs soaking wet, Lonny's mug shot was that of an acne scarred punk with dark curly hair and a series of dark tattoos located along his neck, shoulders, chest and arms. The wife beater he was wearing when the photo was taken was covered in what I presumed to be puke, but it was hard to tell. According to the record, Lonny owned a 1997 Black Jeep Wrangler, and his last known address was Apt 124, Golden Hills Drive, Hopkinsville, Florida. The file contained everything I needed to find him: address, finger prints, social security number, known associates, everything. But most importantly it confirmed that he was the man I was looking for.

Most people think juvenile records are sealed automatically when someone turns 18, but that's not the case in Florida. In Florida, you have to petition the court to have your juvenile record sealed. But doing that won't prevent government organizations like the military, law enforcement, or the courts from gaining access to your information when they want to. Which is why I was able to glean all kinds of interesting details on Lonny's family history from this one record. His folks divorced when he was three. His mother, an addict (gambling and booze), had died from an overdose of heroin when he was twelve, and Lonny had had multiple run-ins with the law since he turned sixteen. He'd bounced in and out of foster care until finally aging out of the system. Yeah, life had given Lonny a shitty stick to hold onto, just like a lot of other kids in his situation.

Skinny, scared, poor, and poorly raised, Lonny reminded me of myself when I was a kid. My Dad split on my Mom and me when I was three years old too, leaving us high and dry in sunny California. He said my Mom's drinking and pot use is what drove him away, but in truth, he just couldn't be bothered to support a family and raise a kid because doing so would have cut into his skirt chasing free time. I knew this because my Dad's latest ex-wife (his fourth) sent me a letter telling me that he had been cheating on her too. After my Dad split, my Mom slipped from one bad relationship into the next before eventually being committed to a rehab center in Montana and finally getting her act together. So yeah, Lonny and I had a few things in common. I even sympathized with his plight, but that wasn't going to stop me from killing him. At some point you have to stop sympathizing with someone and call a spade a spade. Lonny was a coward and a killer. His family history, no matter how bad, didn't excuse his decision to get drunk and kill my wife. He could have followed a different path, but he chose not to. He chose to drink himself silly, and then he chose to get behind the wheel of a three-thousand-pound weapon and risk his life and the lives of those around him. He deserved to die, but my wife didn't. I needed to get going. I needed to kill Lonny before he killed someone else's spouse, or child, or both.

According to the file Lonny had been arrested twice for driving drunk, and currently had a suspended license. But instead of doing jail time, someone had stepped in and done him a solid, arranging for him to get off with probation and time served. The arrest reports listed the street locations where Lonny's DUI busts occurred. I did a quick map quest for those locations on my phone and I was able to determine that each of his arrests had occurred within a few blocks of a local dive bar called the "Rusty Nail," which just happened to be located a mile from his last known address. It looked like Lonny had decided to fan out and drink someplace else the night he hit my wife. She just happened to be in the wrong place at the wrong time. Fate was sick that way.

Looking at the map on my phone, I couldn't help noticing the presence of what looked like a sidewalk leading along the street from the Rusty Nail to Lonny's apartment complex. Jesus! Why didn't this moron walk to the bar that night and save everyone the trouble!

I did a check of the bar's website, and it offered a video streaming feature so prospective customers could see how busy the place was and decide if they wanted to go there to join the party. Most bars in Florida had quickly disabled this service once they started getting customer complaints that their spouses could see them partying, possibly with someone other than their spouse, and raise holy hell. But the Rusty Nail didn't seem to care, which worked to my advantage, because now I could use it to spot Lonny. With any luck, Lonny would make an appearance and save me having to go knock on his door.

Once I finished my sandwich, I stuffed the file in under my arm and walked out to my car. I had decided to stop worrying about Lonny's troubled childhood and focus on getting the job done. When I got to Hopkinsville, I drove directly to Lonny's apartment. I did a quick cruise through the apartment parking lot to orient myself. I was surprised to see Lonny's black Jeep parked in the back of the complex, partially covered with a blue tarp. Anyone with half a lick of sense would have either sold or junked their ride the first chance they got. If Lonny was trying to hide his jeep, he didn't do a good job. Perhaps Lonny felt guilty about he did and he wanted to be caught? To be honest, I wasn't too interested in finding Lonny's car. I already knew how you'd been killed. If this was a different case, I'd be more than happy to canvas all of the local parking lots, used car dealerships, and junk yards in a fifty-mile radius of Lonny's last known address to try and find it. But I wasn't trying to find Lonny's Jeep.

Contrary to popular belief, cars don't always suffer major damage when they hit a pedestrian, not unless the pedestrian is thrown onto the hood or the windshield. You'd be surprised how easy it is to kill someone with a car, all you have to do is line the Jeep's reinforced bumper up right and the person you hit will just collapse forward onto their face as your car drives over them, crushing them with your wheels. So I didn't expect to see a whole lot of damage to Lonny's Jeep after he hit you, at least nothing he couldn't scrub off with a bucket of bleach and a water hose.

The jeep's doors had been removed, and I could see the steering wheel was secured by a padlock and chain that ran from the floorboards up and through the spokes in the steering wheel. Whoever had done this obviously didn't want the vehicle to be moved. Judging from the amount of pollen that had settled on the car, it looked like it hadn't been moved for at least 24 hours. But just to be sure, I got out and checked to see if the engine hood was warm to touch. The weather forecast called for rain later that night, and the skies were filled with dark clouds so I didn't have to worry about the car hood being warm from sitting out in the sun all day. It was stone cold, so I knew it hadn't been moved recently. That was good. That meant Lonny was either in his apartment, or he was at the bar. All I had to do was wait him out.

I made a quick pass through Lonny's apartment building to see if he was home. I wasn't really prepared to confront him right there and then, so I did my best to keep a low profile as I walked through the building, past his apartment door and then back out the other side. Cheap apartment complexes like the one Lonny lived in were often poorly secured and maintained. The majority of people who lived there were transients, people who were there for a short time before moving on, so it wouldn't be unusual to see someone new walking around. Besides, Lonny didn't know me from Adam, so I didn't have to worry about him recognizing me when we ran into each other.

As I passed his apartment door I couldn't help overhearing what sounded like a major argument between two or more people. Maybe Lonny and his old lady were having it out? His file didn't list a girlfriend as a known associate, but that didn't mean he didn't have one. Was that the sound of a man's voice? It sounded familiar. Did I know the person he was talking to? Panic overcame me for the briefest of moments as I tried to figure out who was in Lonny's apartment and why. Was I too late? Was it the police, where they here to arrest Lonny? Damn it! I knew that voice from somewhere; but for the life of me I couldn't remember who it belonged to. I needed to get moving again before someone got suspicious or worse yet, Lonny and/or his angry friend came storming out the front door and right into me. But it was hard to get moving again. The sounds coming from Lonny's apartment had sent a shock of adrenaline through my body, stopping me in mid stride, making it impossible to move or think clearly. I had stopped breathing. My flight or fight responses had kicked in, throwing my body into survival mode. My vision tunneled and my head started to pound from the sudden spike of energy and lack of oxygen. At that moment I felt like I was standing stark naked in the middle of a football field during a homecoming game. But before I could get moving, I needed to regain control of my breath, which was coming in short halting gasps.

I was trying to avoid dragging anyone else into this crappy situation if I could help it. I forced my body to move forward, placing one heavy step after the other until I had cleared Lonny's door and the door next to it. After that, it was walking just a few more feet and I would be through the building and standing on the walkway located on the other side and another parking lot.

I spotted the police cruiser sitting in a parking spot on the other side of the building as I stepped out onto the walkway. Fascinating, most apartment buildings paid cops to park their cruisers in their parking lots at night as a means to scare away potential hooligans and discourage bad behavior. Arranging to have a police cruiser parked at your complex was the equivalent of placing a scarecrow out in the middle of a cornfield, and it worked just about as well. That is to say, not at all. But this cop car was different because instead of being parked in the front by the manager's office where the apartment management team could keep an eye on it, this one was parked in a spot reserved for residents. It was at this point that I realized why the cops hadn't arrested Lonny – he was being protected by one of them. Fug! This meant I was going to have to improvise. They say no plan survives initial contact with the enemy, and it looked this one wasn't going to either. I needed to rethink how I could get at Lonny without involving his protector, which meant I needed to catch him out on his own somewhere between the apartment complex and the bar. So I just kept on walking out of the apartment complex and down the sidewalk towards the Rusty Nail.

The collapse of the housing bubble hit Florida pretty hard. The neighborhood I was walking through was no exception. Most of the houses I walked by needed to be repaired and several of them were actually boarded up presumably after being abandoned by both the former occupants and the banks that owned them. Empty lots were interspersed between the occupied and unoccupied homes, indicating that the house that used to stand there had been torn down, or never built. Someone with a sense of humor had decided to convert one of the larger of the empty lots into a little park, complete with handmade sign that said: Welcome to Prosperity Park – Please Do Not Feed the Animals, and a smiley face. The sign had been placed at the property's edge, close to the sidewalk and the street where it could be clearly seen. A rusty metal bench and broken bird fountain located at the far end of the lot, which had since been surrounded by weeds and a particularly aggressive form of wild bushes, completed the look of total despair that had overcome the neighborhood. I entered the 'park' via a six-foot-long section of concrete walkway that led up to the where the house's foundation would have begun had it been built. The concrete path transitioned to a dirty path that led over to the where the bench and fountain were set up. The area was obviously a local hangout for the neighborhood's kids and the homeless, as evidenced by the amount of empty Mad Dog 20/20 bottles and cardboard beds strewn haphazardly throughout the tall grass and surrounding bushes. If I cared to look hard enough, I would probably find a bunch of used condoms and rusty needles lying on the ground by my feet, but I didn't really care, so I didn't bother looking. Instead, I decided to suspend disbelief for a few moments, and take a little break by the bench, where I could smoke a cigarette or two or four (after all, cancer was no longer a major concern for me) and wait and see what developed.

As evening approached the sky darkened, the wind picked up, and a heavy rain began to fall. I quickly relocated to the porch of one of the nearby abandoned houses where I could stay relatively dry and still keep an eye on the sidewalk and the street without being observed. I didn't know what I was going to do if Lonny went flashing by in a cab, except improvise some more. From time to time I checked the Rusty Nail's video feed to see if Lonny had made it there without being seen, he hadn't, so I assumed he was still at his apartment. I also assumed Lonny would eventually get tired of his friend's company and head towards the Rusty Nail. That's the thing about addicts, they are predictable and they'd use any excuse to get what they want, so I had no doubt Lonny would make an appearance at some point in the evening. That's what my Mom would do. Thirty minutes later, my patience was rewarded and I spotted Lonny heading towards me and the Rusty Nail.

I stepped off of the porch as Lonny walked up to me, flashed my PI credentials at him and said: "Hi Lonny, let's have a little chat in the park, shall we?" Lonny scanned me quickly, and looked like he was about to try and make a break for it, but he quickly changed his mind when I kicked him in the groin. With Lonny subdued, I dragged him down the sidewalk to the little concrete path where I delivered a second kick to his chest, partly because it felt good to do it and mainly because I wanted to make sure I had his full attention. I was about to shine my boots with his groin again, when he started spluttering at me. "You...bastard...do you know....who... my dad... is..."

Bingo! I punctuated my reply with another kick, and said, "I don't care if your dad is a cop or the queen of Sheba, Lonny. You will either answer my questions or I am going to beat you to death, understood?"

Lonny cringed every time I moved, reflexively jerking his head back whenever he thought I was going to hit him again, so I backed off a little and waited for him to catch his breath before I started peppering him with questions.

"Okay Lonny, here's the million-dollar question, convince me you're telling the truth and I'll set you free, lie to me and you will wish you hadn't. Clear?"

"Clear...anything... just stop kicking me." He was still speaking in gasps, but that was okay with me. I just needed him to answer a couple of questions and this would all be done.

"Okay. How long has he been covering for you?" That is when I learned about Lonny's police connection. Driven by guilt, Lonny's dad, the cop, had tried to find the son he abandoned nineteen years ago, and he had used his law enforcement connections to find him, to quash any record of Lonny's illicit behavior, and make amends for abandoning him all those years ago. Everything Lonny told me jived with what I either knew or suspected. It was just pure bad luck that Lonny's dad also happened to be one of the officers assigned to investigate my wife's death, and tasked with informing me about your death. If he'd done his job, you might still be alive, and I wouldn't be here right now. But it did happen, and now there was only one thing left for me to do. "Okay Lonny, I believe you are telling me the truth. I just need you to answer one more question."

"Okay..."

"Why did you run away from that accident two nights ago?"

"What accident? I don't know what you are talking about...when my old man hears about this he is going to give you hell for hitting me- guhhhuh!" Lonny's lips split open the moment I hit him with my fist, choking off any further threats or complaints that he might make.

"Now Lonny, you were doing so well telling me the truth. Why did you make me do that? I told you I wouldn't accept being lied to." I hit him again for emphasis, punctuating each of my sentences with a punch or a kick depending on what was easier at the time. "Besides, I saw you running away that night Lonny." Smack! "There was a camera set up where you hit her Lonny." Thud! "I saw you stop, and I saw you run away. So there really is no sense in you trying to bullshit me on this point Lonny." Whack! "Just assume I already know 90% of the truth and that this is a test of your ability to fill in the missing 10%, okay." I delivered a final kick to his spine before stopping. "Think of it as a confession, you know about confession don't you Lonny? Good boy. Now Lonny, don't pass out on me. I'll only hurt you again if you do."

"Okay, okay... just don't hurt me... I ran because I was scared, man, I didn't know what to do." By this point Lonny was speaking between sobs, groans, and barely whispered "oh mammas," and I was pretty sure he was crying. I wondered if he knew just how close to the end we had come?

"How did your dad find out? Did you tell him?"

"Yes..."

"Was she still alive when you left?"

"I...I didn't' check... I saw the body and I panicked. I just... I just went home and got drunk."

"Was that before or after you called your old man?"

"After."

"And what did he tell you? Lonny, what did he tell you?

"He told me to go home."

"Thank you Lonny. You did very well. Now, before we say goodbye, would you mind doing me one more favor?"

"What?"

"Call your dad and tell him where you are and that you are in trouble."

"Why...Okay... don't hit me... This is only going to end badly."

I replied with "probably," but Lonny was too busy talking on the phone with his old man to hear me say it. There was no point in prolonging Lonny's misery any further, so I shot him in the head twice when he hung up. He never saw it coming. Standing there, I couldn't help thinking now would be a good time to run away. But that wasn't my style. So I slipped my gun back into my pocket, lit another cigarette and waited for the cops to arrive. I was waiting for one cop in particular. I just hoped he was willing to do the right thing.

2016

Max Parker
The Missing Prescription Pad

Jason Brown

Prologue

Same dream again. Evelyn is gagged and tied to a decaying post on a sinking pier. All I can do is watch while my feet are cemented to the harbor floor. This time Photi is on the pier. He is trying to help Evelyn escape. As the water fills my lungs, I wake and relax my jaw. I am covered in sweat. I can feel loose granules of teeth in the pits of my molars. Bruxism is apparently caused by eating sugar before bed (along with a host of other reasons). I will have to cut out the late night Sour Patch Kids.

The sound of sirens outside my window reminds me how insignificant one man's nightmare is in Baltimore. The city feels more ruthless everyday. When I was growing up, there was an order to crime in the city. Nowadays, it's every gun for himself and the cops can barely keep up with the parking violations. Besides the jobs I do are too dirty for the boys in blue.

Believe it or not, I used to be one of the good guys. Sometimes I still am. I respect what the law claims to represent; a protection of individual freedom. It just seems the system has lost sight of that. It's nothing but an industry now. Trust me, I worked for the DEA for nine years. The last four I spent undercover, and that's where everything went wrong. I can't say I was entirely innocent, but I didn't do half of what I stood accused of. Needless to say, I got some time. But all that's over now. I have found my own way to set a small part of the world right: the forgotten sector. It has its rewards.

* * * * *

Photi told me last night (after three hours of beer and darts) that I am a desperate man's last resort. I specialize in those the police refuse to help.

The ex-con, the illegal immigrant, the wanted criminal; the discreet disenfranchised if you would. What is most rewarding about these clients is my ability to gouge their pockets. I also wind up with a number of cases that people are afraid to present to the official authorities. They come to me when their problem needs discretion. I turn down some, but for the most part I just price out the bad cases. Sometimes I get myself stuck this way.

For example: two weeks ago, Big Charlie (a heroin smuggler and a union longshoreman) walks into my office and asks me to find fifteen kilos of raw dope. Usually, I would say no; but Big Charlie doesn't like that word, and he is not someone to upset. So, I did the math on fifteen kilos (turns out to be worth over a million bucks), and decided that a hundred grand would probably be twice what Charlie was willing to pay. Especially considering that I get half up front, regardless of the outcome. This bastard says "you got it- just find my shit!" Now, I am nursing a bullet hole that went clean through my left shoulder. Fuckin' with Big Charlie. Although I did buy a really nice yacht from a friend's chop shop with the hundred grand. Got it docked down in Canton. I plan on moving the office there as soon as this shoulder heals up. Currently, my office is set up in a slum section of Park Heights, over by Pimlico racetrack. I live in a loft above it, pretty much all I could afford when I got out of prison last year. Great for balancing my income with horse racing on the slow days.

Who the hell is knocking on my door at this hour!

"Hello?"

"Is this Max Parker's office?" The voice suggests femininity.

"Yes, but it's a little late; office closed over six hours ago."

"Max, it's me- Evelyn."

How did I not recognize that voice? Suddenly, a wave of nostalgia comes rushing over me. I open the door and her red hair spills into my office like a wildfire in search of oxygen. The rest of her ivory essence follows subtly. Her big green doe eyes catch me off guard.

"Oh, Max, it's been much too long."

"I was just thinkin' the same thing. How ya been Ev?"

"I been better, things got all screwed up when you went down. Honestly, I have wanted to come see you since I heard you were out over six months ago, but I have been too scared. I kept imagining that you wouldn't want to see me- that I was all part of your cover, that Max Parker could never really love a loser like me." Evelyn is about to fall to pieces, I can hear it in her voice.

"Listen babe, my life undercover really started to take over my actual life and that had a lot to do with you. I tried to remain objective and do my job, but you changed everything for me. And you know what, seeing you here now makes it almost worth it. C'mere Ev." We embrace and there is a sense of relief that neither of us have felt in years. We kiss and every time that we have ever kissed happens all over again. Every sensation I had forgotten is awakened. Every spark I worked so hard to smoother, flares like the fourth of July. I recoil, afraid of the repercussions. Evelyn always comes with baggage.

"So, what's the deal sugar? You need something else or just come over to see me?"

Evelyn says nothing. She just smiles and grabs my cock. So much for resisting. We ascend the spiral staircase to my loft above the office. It is a whirlwind of dirty clothes and wrinkled papers. Evelyn doesn't seem to mind as she clears a spot on the bed. We take each other places we wish we had never left. Evelyn eventually falls asleep on my chest, curled into my side. I forgot how radiantly warm she is.

The morning brings boisterous knocking that Evelyn and I are not prepared for. That knock, it's either the police or Photi.

"C'mon Max, open the door- it's just me."

Photi, great. The police would be more welcome at this point. Photi is my partner, but mostly we just drink and play darts together. We crossed paths tracking a wanted criminal about six months ago. Photi is a bounty hunter, and I was "locating" someone of interest for a client. After I realized that he could be bought, Photi and I became dear friends. Last time he was at the office, it was the same routine. Twenty minutes after the office is supposed to open and I am half-naked with company. That's all I need is for him to threaten to pull his license again. Technically, the whole business is his because it's impossible to get a proper investigator's license with a record. Fortunately, Photi's bounty hunter license serves the same purpose. On paper, I am just his greeter.

"Coming old friend, slept in again. Sorry about that."

"Is there someone upstairs? I hear the floor creaking and the water running,"

"Quite the detective you are turning into, Photi."

"Who is the lucky girl today?"

"Evelyn Vanderbilt."

"You mean the one that you called mentally unstable and asked me to keep you away from?"

"No that must have been someone else, Photi!" I interject quickly and loudly.

Evelyn comes down the stairs in nothing but a t-shirt and red panties. Her white thighs gleam in the morning light. Photi and I look away long enough for her to descend and retain a shred of modesty.

"Photi, Evelyn; Evelyn, this is my partner, Photi."

"Guess Max has already told you all about me, huh?" Evelyn says with pursed lips to boot.

"Just that you two used to run together I think. Max don't gossip too much."

Thank you, Photi. He must want me to pay for lunch or something.

"So, Evelyn, I have some business to discuss with Photi, should I call you a cab?"

"Sure, just give me a minute to dress, and, oh yeah, there was one other thing."

Here it comes, I knew there would be a catch.

"What is it dear?"

"Big Charlie wanted me to thank you for doin' a good job."

"Oh yeah, so you're his new thank you card huh? I will have to remember that."

"It ain't like that Max, he told me you had been shot and I really felt bad for you. I told you already how difficult this has been for me. Don't make it any harder please Max. Charlie takes care of me."

"I'm sure he does, babe."

"I did this for you Max! Quit bein' such a jerk, what'd ya think I fuck every guy he asks me to?"

"No sugar, probably just the handsome ones."

Evelyn begins to cry. What am I saying to her? I am such a jerk. She is doing the same thing I do, whatever it takes to survive comfortably. That's partially my fault for conditioning the girl to a lifestyle well beyond her means. Now she works for Big Charlie. Out of all the redheads in Baltimore, he had to pick mine. The hole in my shoulder begins to throb. I am suddenly nauseous and no longer interested in lunch. I pick up the phone and call Evelyn a cab.

Photi and I go out for lunch, my treat. I owe him at least that much. If it weren't for his timely arrival, who knows how long Evelyn and I would have played out that unending charade?

"Watcha thinkin' about? Her, huh?"

"Photi, you know me well."

"So to get this straight, she's been workin' for Big Charlie since you went down?"

"Yes, but going down implies I did something wrong. Can we just say since I was fired?"

"Sure, but gettin' fired usually don't involve doin' five years in prison."

"It was only five on paper, I was out in half of that with my exemplary behavior." My phone vibrates and fortunately averts my attention from recalling the twenty-nine months I spent locked up in Hazelton, WV.

"Hello."

"Hey it's Charlie, how'd ya like seein' your old broad again?"

"Yeah, she sure is somethin', huh?"

"Well, listen I know you are healing up still, but I got a real easy one for ya in Delaware if you're interested."

"Define easy."

"Okay, this friend of mine, Dr. Titan, is a pain doctor and let's just say he gives people what they want. So, of course, the feds have been looking into his practice for years. Suddenly, he starts noticing these prescriptions coming back that he never wrote. He realizes some junkie has stolen a prescription pad and is forging his signature for all kinds of shit. Fortunately, the feds haven't picked up on this, but Doc knows it is only a matter of time. What we need is someone to discreetly find the pad and return it."

"Well, as always, it comes down to the price tag."

"Right, I told him you were expensive and he said that he will pay whatever it takes to save his practice."

"How much are we talkin'?"

"I can give you ten grand here, and he can settle with you on the rest when you get the pad. You will have to work out the details when you get to Delaware."

"The case could take up to a week depending on how long it takes me to find the patient who stole the pad."

"I never said it was a patient, Max."

"I know this, but an employee would be too smart and who else goes in the back at a pain specialist's beside patients? A patient's family member perhaps, either way-- I am looking for a patient."

"Listen, a week of your time is a lot I understand, but this won't end up like the last case-- I promise. I will write ya a check and have it delivered to your office today. Then I will call Dr. Titan and tell him you will be there tomorrow. The two of you can work out the details in person."

"One last thing Charlie, you still owe me ten grand for the GBMC medical bills for this bullet I took."

"Okay, ten and ten make twenty, you got it. Take care Max."

I push the red "End" button on my phone and turn to Photi. My shoulder is thumping like the pulse of a frightened rabbit.

"Something weird about this one, Photi."

"You aren't seriously considering taking another of Big Charlie's jobs, are you? Max, C'mon. He stole your woman, got you shot, and you run off to help him?"

"Usually I would price him out or gouge him. But he has awakened my curiosity, and I would like to talk to this Dr. Titan. Not to mention I am almost out of my Roxies, and this shoulder is throbbing. Besides, Big Charlie is up to something and I have to know what it is."

"How do you know he is 'up to something'?"

"He has contacted me three times in two weeks, which is unprecedented. I have sparked his interest for some reason. I have to see this through, Photi. Try to understand, there is still a lot I haven't figured out about my arrest. It seems that Evelyn and Charlie could help shed light on what exactly happened three years ago. This is more personal than anything. Don't want to get you mixed up in any of this, in case things get messy."

"Max, you know I don't shy from danger, just don't do anything stupid. I don't mind risking my life for the right cause."

"I don't need to you take any risks over this saga, Photi. All I need you to do is stay close to the office in case I need you to look anything up. I'll go to Delaware tomorrow and find out what Charlie's scheming. You up for some darts tonight?"

"With a hole in your shoulder?"

"I take back everything I have said in favor of your deductive abilities. I'm right-handed Photi. The bullet went through my left shoulder!"

"I know you're right-handed, just couldn't remember where you got shot."

"So you're just unsympathetic, that's a relief."

The next day I stagger through the beer bottles and darts strewn about the floor of the office. My shoulder is throbbing. I find the bottle of Roxicet just in time. One left. The refill is two weeks away. Gonna have to get to Delaware and talk to Dr. Titan, soon.

"Photi, I'm headed to Delaware. You all right cleaning up and watching things for a few days?"

"I told you, I got this. No problem."

With that, Photi hits the snooze button and rolls back over on the couch. I step out into a warm spring breeze that refreshes my outlook. Two hours to Delaware and then this shoulder stops throbbing. I open my Volvo up and get there in ninety minutes.

The office is a rancher with a wooden sign out front. I park and make my way into the rural temple of relief.

"Hello, Max Parker here to see Dr. Titan."

"Have a seat, he will call you back, Mr. Parker."

The receptionist's name tag says Alice. She is definitely in Wonderland. This office is a zoo of reprobates and delinquents in search of their next fix. A few people look like they have legitimate pain, but most of this sweat-clothes covered motley crew are here for the high.

"Mr. Parker, please come back."

Dr. Titan is a short man with a tan complexion. His bald head and stoic smile make him appear intelligent, but there is something off about him. He escorts me back to his office.

"Have a seat, Max-- you don't mind that I call you Max, do you?"

"No, Max is fine. I guess Charlie told you I was comin'?"

"He did. I understand that we need to work out a payment arrangement before you begin trying to locate the missing prescription pad."

"Yes, about the payment. Well, I took this bullet a few weeks back for our friend Big Charlie and the doctor in Baltimore didn't give me enough to kill the pain. I ran out of pills this morning. Think we could work something out?"

"This sounds very feasible. What would you like to have?"

He begins fumbling with a locked drawer on his desk and I sense relief is near.

"Those will work."

"These are Fentanyl patches; they are very strong."

"I know what they are. How many of them can you spare?"

"I will give you twenty now and I can send you another twenty after the job is completed. They are worth over two thousand dollars on the street altogether. I will also hand you a check for five grand when you hand me the prescription pad. With Charlie's ten, that is seventeen grand. Do we have a deal?"

"I guess so, since this patch is already stuck to my shoulder."

"Good, where shall we start?"

I have his secretary compose a list of all the patients that came in the week that the pad went missing. I call Photi.

"Are you still at the office?"

"No, just over at the track though. Why, what's up?"

"Can you still run the IntegraScan background checks?"

"Yeah, back at the office. They charge per inquiry, how many you got?" Photi hesitantly asks.

"Shit, he saw over fifty patients the week the pad went missing."

"At twenty bucks a pop, this could take a thousand dollars and yield nothing Max."

"It's my only shot Photi. I hate to ask you to possibly waste hours of your time, but I really need to know if any of these patients have a record. I will reimburse you the twenty for each inquiry, along with a thousand for looking. If you find something good, I will split the five grand the doctor gave me with you."

"How can I say no to that? Especially considering I just blew nine hundred on a "sure bet Trifecta" that missed. I'll be at the office in five minutes, call you as soon as I find something."

"Thanks Photi, I owe you big."

I check into a Red Roof Inn, waiting for Photi to turn something up. They have an Indian buffet next to the lobby. After some lamb vindaloo and a mango lassi, I find my way to room four twenty-one. Just as I lie down, my phone begins to vibrate. I hope this is Photi.

"Hello."

"Hey Max, it's Evelyn."

"Hey there, how are ya?"

"I am fine, what are you up to?"

"Just waiting for Photi to call me with some info, on a job in Delaware. But you probably already knew that."

"No, Charlie don't tell me much."

"Yeah, well the less you know the better off you are."

"I guess. I won't hold you up long, just wanted to tell you that I had a really good time the other night." With that there is a click and the phone goes dead. I was about to say that I enjoyed it as well. Photi calls just as I was drifting to sleep. The digital alarm clock says nine p.m. Those patches are strong.

"Hey Photi, tell me something good."

"As groggy as you sound, you must already have something good."

"Just some Fentanyl patches from the good doctor, a little stronger than I remember."

"Jesus, be careful Max. People die from that stuff. Anyway, I found one kid with an interesting record, after about thirty inquiries. Adam Deveaux, convicted of prescription forgery when he was eighteen. That was almost two years ago, but he was locked up for nineteen months. He just got out about five months ago, lives in an apartment complex in Wilmington. I got an address, I'll text it to you."

"Thanks a million Photi. I owe you as usual. I was hoping you could do me one last favor and run Big Charlie through there. I know it won't yield much, but I would like to know if there is a pattern to his charges. He usually beats 'em, but they should still be listed on his record. I might find some dirt useful if there are any problems with Charlie."

"Charles Monroe, listed union worker. Already found his date of birth. I'll hit you back after I analyze his background check. Be careful out there Max."

"Thanks again Photi, talk to ya soon."

Thanks to GPS, I find Adam's building easily. His room is on the third floor, I take the stairs to be discreet. Room 321, it's a countdown. I knock softly.

"Who is it?" The voice sounds groggy and monotone, definitely my man.

"Just doing a survey, you got a minute?"

"I guess, just make it quick, I got a meeting in an hour." He says this while opening the door. I push my way in and he gets real startled.

"What the hell dude? Get the fuck outta here?"

"Listen, Adam, you are in a fuck load of trouble so I suggest you sit down, shut up, and cooperate. If I can swing it, you won't be in jail tonight; just detox."

"Jail? Detox? What the fuck are you talking about dude?"

"Dr. Titan knows you took his prescription pad. He hired me to find you and I found you quick. The feds are close behind, no doubt. If I can get the pad back to the good doctor, I may be able to convince him not to call the police. If I do this for you, you gotta do something for me."

"This is fuckin' bullshit dude!"

"Should I just call the cops now?"

"Fuck you!"

"Listen to me Adam, you don't want to go down this road. I have lived up and down it and it's treacherous the whole way."

I am such a fucking hypocrite right now, but what else can I say to the kid? Hey, keep getting' high for the rest of your life, so you end up like me one day! Fuck, I hate it when I care.

Adam puts his head in his hands and begins sobbing in a way I can relate to. I tell him everything will be fine. It's probably a lie.

"I have been to Kirkwood once, it wasn't that bad I guess." Adam finally says through the tears.

"Three days and I am out. I have probation on Tuesday, so that should work. Just let me grab some things. And here is the pad."

Adam suddenly seems filled with energy and ambition. He unlocks a small lockbox and hands over what is left of the prescription pad. It is only about a third full, but something tells me that Adam might not have made it through those last thirty pages. The hollow twinkle in his eye says he is well aware of this.

I walk him into Kirkwood Detox Center to make sure that he checks himself in. I tell him to leave the crime behind and head back to the doctor. People have to start doing right for themselves at some point. I hope it's Adam's time.

I get to Dr. Titan's office late, but he is still there waiting for me. I texted him and told him I had the pad hours ago. I hand him what is left of the pad and he hands me my check. I explain that Adam is getting some help and advise the doctor not to see him anymore. I am ready to get back to Baltimore.

I get back to the office around midnight. When I open the door and reach for the light switch, nothing happens.

"Photi, you here?"

Silence. Something is wrong. I pull a lighter from my pocket and the flame illuminates the mess. There are papers all over the place. The computer has been ripped out. Finally, I make out the shape of a body behind the desk. Fuck me, it's Photi. His body is already stiffening. Two shots, one in the chest, one in the head. I know this was Big Charlie. But how did he know that Photi was checking him out? Evelyn! She must have bugged the office when I had her over the other night. Charlie has a habit of eavesdropping on everyone he can. This is all my fault, I got

Photi killed. Only one way to make this right, gotta go after Evelyn and Charlie. I call and report a shooting at the office. I'd like to stay and explain, but I will be detained for twenty-four hours if I'm even at the crime scene. Murder scenes and felons don't mix. Besides, I gotta find Charlie if there's gonna be any justice for Photi's death.

I head for the harbor. Big Charlie has a yacht down there, hopefully he is on it. I stop off at a storage area registered to Photi. It's where I keep my gun. Now that I am a felon, I can't go around packin' all the time. Only when I know I will need it.

Once at the dock, I quietly sneak onto Charlie's boat. I can hear Evelyn laughing below the deck. I bust into their cabin and point the gun at Charlie.

"I want answers, big man, now."

"Max, what the hell's this about?"

"You have been up to something for the past month and now Photi is dead."

"I had nothin' to do with that Max. Evelyn will tell you, we been on the boat since last night."

"It's the truth Max, me and Charlie been here on the boat all day."

"Tell me something Evelyn, how long did it take after I got arrested for you to start trickin' for dope again?"

"Actually, Max, I was trickin' her out when you went down. You just didn't know about it."

"Charlie, you promised you wouldn't tell him. Oh Max, I'm so sorry. I wanted to stay clean and be happy with you, but the clinic wasn't enough. I started getting high behind your back and before I knew it, Charlie had me strung out."

Things were finally starting to make sense. I was trying to save Evelyn, but all I did was ruin my own life. The prosecution used my relationship with Evelyn to seal the deal on my case. I always thought it would be worth it if I got out and she was doing better. Reality has a cruel way of shattering our dreams.

"See Max, junkies like Evelyn never change. People like you always get used. And I always get what I want. Shame for you, I wanted Evelyn so bad."

"So bad that you hired me just to have someone kill me? And when that didn't work, you sent Evelyn over to bug the office so you could keep tabs on me. Then you send me off to Delaware in order to kill off my partner, essentially shutting me down as well. Everything is crystal clear to me now Charlie."

"Max, what evidence do you have for any of this?"

"None, but I do have a gun pointed at you. I was thinkin' we would skip the trial and go straight to the sentencing."

"Max, you aren't thinkin' clearly. You are just upset and irrational. Even if you are right, where does killin' me get you?"

"Well, it will make me feel a little better about Photi bein' dead. I don't know if you pulled the trigger or not, but I know you had him killed. I can't let that slide, Charlie."

I take aim right between his eyes and blow a hole in the middle of Big Charlie's head. He falls backward, onto his bed. Blood soaks his white satin bedding. Evelyn is screaming. She will always be a whore. I really thought I loved her. Time to put her down.

"Sorry Evelyn, this is the only way."

I hug her close, sticking the nose of my gun into the back of her neck. I fire upwards through the top of her head. I feel splatters of blood and small chunks of flesh on my cheek. I gotta get the fuck outta here. Fortunately, my yacht is only a few piers away.

I reach my vessel before I see the lights from the cop cars over on Charlie's dock. I quietly head out into the harbor. Plan on heading south, gonna have to lay low for a while after this mess. Got about fifty grand and eighteen patches left. That should be enough to get me where I need to go.

2012

About the Authors

Jason Brown was born in Chicago Heights, Illinois in 1980. He graduated from Shepherd University in 2005 with a Bachelor of Arts and Loyola University with a Master of Arts in Liberal Studies in 2014. He is currently pursuing a Master of Fine Arts in Creative Writing with a concentration in Memoir at University of Baltimore.

David Dougherty is emeritus professor of English and Liberal Studies at Loyola University Maryland. For a decade he directed Loyola's Master of Modern Studies, leading the transition to its current status as Graduate Program in Liberal Studies. The author of three books and editor of two others, he's published nearly 80 essays on modern and postmodern writers, literary and political history, and baseball. Detective writers he's written about include Raymond Chandler, Laura Lippman, Ross Macdonald, and Rex Stout.

Dan Helwig graduated from Susquehanna University last millennium. He shares a small farm near Hershey, Pennsylvania with a half-dozen chickens, a couple of goats, some cats that won't go away, and a dog named Dixie. He also serves as Vice President of Advancement at Lebanon Valley College.

Helen Hufford, a native Baltimorean, attended Loyola University as an undergraduate and returned to earn her master's degree in the Liberal Studies program in 2012. She is the English Department Chair at Mount de Sales Academy in Catonsville, Maryland where she enjoys teaching AP English literature, British literature, creative writing, and film study.

Carl Kinkel is a retired U.S. Army Warrant Officer and veteran of both Iraq wars and the war in Afghanistan. When he is not writing papers for his Master of Liberal Studies classes at Loyola University Maryland, he enjoys building war games miniatures and dreaming of one day being an Orioles season ticket holder. He, his wife, and his five-year old daughter live in Baltimore City under the benevolent oversight of their cat, Eli.

Jennifer Louden was born in N.J. and has lived in the Baltimore/D.C. area for the past 15 years and now considers this area home. Since graduating from college she has worked in higher education, traveling around the country recruiting students. Her husband and she love to run (much like Nina Langston) and you will often find them out on the paths early in the morning.

Chris Panzarella greatly enjoyed writing his story, and he looks forward to continuing to write in the future. A high school Math teacher, Chris works in Howard County, Maryland and lives in Washington, DC with his fiancé and two tabby cats.

Jonathan Richmond grew up in Morris County, New Jersey. He earned his undergraduate degree in History and Secondary Education from the University of Delaware and his Master's in Liberal Studies from Loyola University Maryland. A lifelong teacher, he currently teaches Economics and Philosophy at Western School of Technology and Environmental Science in Catonsville, Maryland.

He lives with his two sons, Matthew and Evan, in White Marsh, Maryland.

Nicole Stout is a mother, wife, teacher of English, bona fide Jersey Girl, and graduate of the Liberal Studies program at Loyola University. This short story's success is based on the realistic aspects of mobster life it presents, and for their experience with underworld activities and mob related knowledge, she is eternally grateful to the gone but always adored James Condit and, of course, Stephen Marcianti.

Katalin Szoboszlay Navarro is a graduate student in Liberal Studies at Loyola University Maryland. She received her B.A. in English and Theatre Arts from McDaniel College, where she graduated magna cum laude in 2012. Katalin is currently enjoying the newlywed life with her husband in their new home in Howard County, MD.